Tiempo, Texas

by

Max Tyrone Lozano

Beyond Borders Books

Pharr, Texas

ACKNOWLEDGEMENTS

Thank you:

First and foremost, to Thomas Ray Garcia for always believing in this project, which took nearly a decade. You understood this book even before I had time to complete it. With Spirit, my great friend.

Aaron Reyes for the absolutely sick cover art. I only gave you crumbs of themes and symbols; now, I'm proud to know that when people think of Tiempo, two artists will come to mind: William Faulkner and the Omelette Daddy, himself, Mr. Aaron Reyes.

To the rest of my friends, who've let me into their lives graciously. What I have done either in this or a past life to earn your trust and your kindness and your kinship, I don't know, nor do I care to unpack. From *las Charras*, to a defunct university writing group; from the colleagues alongside which I've suffered through turnstile management, to the classmates truly dedicated to making this lonesome crowded wheeling earth better: To these and many more people of high devotion, high life: my unflagging gratitude.

Lastly, to my mom, Alice Trejo, who deserves way more than a line on a page. May this book be the first of many lines dedicated to you.

"I give you the mausoleum of all hope and desire… I give it to you not that you may remember time, but that you might forget it now and then for a moment and not spend all your breath trying to conquer it. Because no battle is ever won he said. They are not even fought. The field only reveals to man his own folly and despair, and victory is an illusion of philosophers and fools."

— William Faulkner, *The Sound and the Fury*

TABLE OF CONTENTS

AWAY NOW:
THE STORY STARTS, AND NO ONE KNOWS WHO'S TELLING IT

Places, much like other things, much like me, look different once you're a distance away from them. Take Tiempo, for example. A place of which some of its inhabitants draw blanks as to its name— which occurs to a select few—and its whereabouts. (I've seen full-grown adults scratch their heads trying to find Tiempo on a map. The elderly don't waste their time.) It's easy to forget things bigger than you are. It's easy to forget Tiempo. Sure, we have a mall; a carnival visits every other season; and we're somewhat close to McAllen, wherever that is. People know McAllen. They go, "Oh yeah, that big thing." I'm not dissing it. They have a lot of good things other neighboring cities don't. Even so, people will remember the more innocuous cities, the more peripheral cities, most of which have image books about them at the library. Those books will depict the sanitized version of history, like no self-respecting Chicano ever cracked-open an Américo Paredes story. Yet, I still can't say with all certainty that we don't share some of the blame. If I can accept that we as individuals have a hand in the narratives that land on the 24-hour news cycles, why can't they save their disparaging words and say once and for all that our violence and our neglect is a result of violence and neglect? I guess what it comes down to is control...

I cannot help but to think of Tiempo.

Nobody knows exactly how it came to be, nor for what reason, and the circumstances of its conception differ from whom you ask. Some say that farmers from other places built houses there to spend time away from their work and families, and that eventually their spouses caught on and, with a face, convinced their significant other to move the family to what is now called Tiempo, in an act of revenge and familial consolidation. The name came after the discovery, as most names come. In many ways, the advent of "Tiempo" made life finite: Whereas before, many stories told of an age of excess under the golden bowl of the sun, now things have names, and families go back at least three generations.

I remember my grandmother told me that the land was given to a son of wealth whose father wanted him to cultivate it as he did his own once during the days of Indian scalping and vast masses of uncharted land. The son did nothing but invite women to his house and sleep with them under starless skies, surrounded by rattlesnake serenades, while his father sent workers with orders to till the land until something grew, regardless of his son's acknowledgment. One day, the son awoke to find his territory populated and busy, the progress of which rustled within the ether of his snores and promiscuity. That's what my grandmother told me, but then again not even my father trusted her, nor did he like her, for that matter.

Eventually they built the road I'm traveling, like a thread running through to the rest of America, the rest of the world. Sitting across the aisle from me, inattentive to the window bearing his faint reflection, is this old, dark-haired man clutching a crucifix to the breast of his burgundy suit, his oily fingers sliding over the gold. He was here before Tiempo. I'm speculating he'll be in that seat alone even after I get to where I'm going.

| * |

As often as people forget it, I will always remember how it looks like under the purple of twilight: how it resembles any other city fleeting from your eyes; how it lingers like an afterthought above reality, flattening and flattening, until the ground ups and swallows it whole. And it stays there for a while, in the belly of the harsh brushlands, underneath the edge of the world, anticipating your visit, and when you do visit (I assume), it might suddenly change, almost as if you ushered in something new. But you didn't. Its people did; and, in a way, the people and the place are the same.

Now, what does that say about me?

As much as it was a place for me, in its own way, Tiempo may have been something of a parent. It treated me like the middle child: that is, with waning indifference. Its constant warmth never seemed inviting to me. It never seemed to care which road I took to get to one place or another—I just got there somehow. It never made an attempt to understand me. Tiempo never apologized when it did me wrong. And at one instant I believe it said to me this: "I am what I am. You want to change me? I raised you. How far will you stretch me? How far do I have to go for you? I lead different lives for other people, and you want me to stop and give you special attention—pure vanity." It may sound a bit crazy, but a childhood in a place can do that to you.

Leaving it, I could trace the way back, the road that turns into the undulating expressway on which my mom took me for midnight rides. And from her car, I could see the city mapped in lights and darkness. And on a rise, I could spot the Tequila Worm for its blinking electrified mascot in fluorescent bottle surveying downtown. The blackness of the sleeping Sunset Mall. The aisle of stoplights down Main Street (all of which agreed with each other), leading to the too-sleeping Pending Circle. My family's house.

Well, it's going to belong to someone else soon. I know I should be sad about losing it, but at a certain point along the way, it stopped being my home.

Home.

Such a strange word. It feels strange, at least. Just the knowing that such a word exists, that other people use it to describe some world between toilet and bed and portrait and kindness and care. The word feels like a memory of experience to me. It's something, but I cannot tell whether it belonged to me or someone else. If ownership can even fall upon it.

As for the events that took place regarding my family, I feel like I haven't given them much thought. I can't tell heads or tails of them. I know I should feel something dreary; and I know that there's something looming over and away, creeping in the back of my skull. I will admit, however, that it interrupts my thoughts from time to time. Parts of me are fooled into thinking that it never actually happened, that the sequence of events and the events, themselves, are a fabrication. (Reminds me of those stories you hear about involving the mysterious disappearance of such-and-such: They have a history until suddenly they're gone, making you question whether that person actually lived or not, whether that history existed or fiction replaces it from that point forward.) I never asked for it. I can say that with all honesty now. It just feels like someone made it happen for me; not that I cheated, but that someone else helped me cheat without my consent. I don't feel any better for it. But I feel good about myself. I know it must sound malicious or ugly. But I do. It's not precisely that I do…

Now that I've managed to escape Tiempo—and I believe

that's the right word for it, "escape"—I can forget about it: forget about the disappearances, forget the culture I never felt welcomed in, forget the fragmentation of self. I want nothing to do with Tiempo. (The dead pixels on my phone completely block the clock. I can't believe I dropped it.) If salvation exists, let mine exist in forgetting.

I'm going to rest my eyes now. (I'm unsure of whether my mind will keep reeling away.) I'll expect to wake up sometime in the morning under some unfamiliar sky in some unfamiliar town with unfamiliar people. With so many variables in my perception, who says I can't be unfamiliar myself?

THE BOOK OF IRREFUTABLE TRUTHS: SETTING THE OLD MAN'S QUALMS ASIDE, THE BOOK CONTINUES

'This I know is true.'

That thought escaped the old man's mind, though not through his thin lips the shape of two old wood planks gently placed together. The thought clung to the air, stale with winter's presence, steeling itself inside the old man's one-bedroom home. Sandwiched between two modernized houses, complete with upstairs additions, in a score of neighboring mid-century real estate updated for a turn-of-the-century market, the home of Old Crow looked like an optical illusion, perhaps tricking the spectator into stepping back and squinting as one might do to a piece of obscure art.

A plane cut through leagues and leagues of midday blue empty of clouds. As the ears of neighborhood pets perked up like antennas, and the kiskadee skittered in the shifting leaves, Old Crow lifted his chin as if to press his ear to the blue domain beyond the shadowy ceiling. He didn't know when the lights went out.

Presently, he stood at the center of the house, at the doorway to the bedroom, now staring across at the window accumulating black oxidation at the bottom edges.

'I came back to write, and now they're all gone.'

He began pacing the whole house—a rather dizzying habit he developed in his late years, dizzying on account of the short walkway and the military-esque gait and about-face in which he conducted this habit. There was a strange pendulum-like quality in his movement. At each turn he would remember the faces and hearts of his friends, now bygone spirits he wished to entertain. Some have moved away, even before he returned to Tiempo; others have passed away. The house he inhabited at one time belonged to a friend who had been gone for decades, now. Where did she go? Was she going to return, as well? Or had she gone into the realm of the fleshless?

Pepe and Idalia, who had inherited the house from their fallen friend, made Old Crow its custodian. They didn't feel right holding onto it after what had happened; this compounded with their shared desire to finally leave the Rio Grande Valley and live on the West

Coast, which meant Old Crow had to manage the house on his own. His parents had long since departed into that unimaginable void, too.

What was her name, the previous owner of this house? The evidence was all around him. But the eyes searched inward as the mouth sounded possible names. The cold chased it away, teasing him all about the house.

His friend's library consisted of handcrafted shelves and heat-warped books, bent after summers with no A/C but what little breeze chanced upon an open window. If he wanted to, he could venture outside to the mailbox. She still collected mail after all these years. He would sometimes glean the gambit of papers she accumulated: mostly advertisements and same-day loan offers. Companies still try to reach into your pockets through the grave, it seemed. There would be a few letters from disparate locations across the U.S. She had traveled to the States when she was a girl with her mother, who had been a Mexican intellectual trying to bridge the academic divide between the two nations. As her mother went from state university to city college, they accrued a number of pen pals who would write to them, many of whom were student protestors demonstrating against the Vietnam War. Old Crow remembered her recalling her mother— Patricia! that's her mother's name!—reading aloud the prose of hippie intellectuals. Her (Patricia's) face, her daughter remembered, would sharpen as talk of theory whittled-down to the soft and warm core of mortality. Their eyes would meet after the last written word. When her mother passed away, the letters still came to her home in Tiempo.

She didn't care to talk politics, but many of the students-turned-regular-nine-to-fivers clung to political engagement as impetus for change, for navigation.

Old Crow knew it was wrong of him to read old letters addressed to her. What else was there to do? In a sense, they brought him glimmers of conversations in which he could vicariously partake.

But today, he scanned the room, foolishly grasping the walls of his memory, which knows before knowing can remember.

Like Old Crow, his friend had led the single life, prioritizing her privacy over most things; she only made use of one sparse bedroom, devoid of decorum, leaving enough space for push-ups and meditations. She had lined the living room walls with portraits of her distant family living in the outskirts of Mexico City, as well as one picture of her shaking hands with Oscar Zeta Acosta a few years before his (Oscar's) disappearance aboard a snowy boat, herself a teenager at the time the photo was taken. The study was lined with bookcases of various literatures and journals, many signed copies of poetry books by Chicano writers. A desk stood adjacent to the window so that when Old Crow took his seat, he could peer outside and behold the driveway, the view of neighboring houses, and the chance passersby.

The outside world didn't captivate him currently, however. The thought occupied him, his eyes fixated on something floating before him, his countenance oscillating between addlement and spriteliness. His wanderings seemed to come in this order: The old man would muster up all his austerity searching for something—a concept or shape in darkness—and he would follow it up, consciously or otherwise, with some lighthearted thought and chase after it.

One thing you will need to know about our character here is that—and he's at this point fully aware of this—he speaks to people who may or may not exist in our physical realm.

This characteristic may not be so detrimental to anyone concerned—especially to the old man. Why, take for instance the previous evening whereupon a late-night excursion to Tiempo's lonely bar, the Tequila Worm, Old Crow seemed to be in high spirits.

'Look at that old crow,' thought Alfredo Quintanilla, the bar's owner whose eyes followed the lively character from one end of the barroom to the other. It was, as Quintanilla had passively, sans the slightest abnegation, noticed over years of dwindling business, a slow evening.

From the perimeters, cacophonous murmurs of conversations between framed photographs of notable guests peaked and petered in the subconscious zone of the walls. Decades of thoughts and alcohol and cigarettes behind glass arranged in surely chaotic order understood their boundaries, for the core of the bar sat in silence. Though largely unpopulated, there was an occupancy of five bar-goers scattered throughout the rows of booths and tables: Quintanilla, Old Crow, and three other customers whose loyalty went without word or even thought. This was what the reserved bar owner, burly and mustached underneath his wide nostrils, saw along with the other occupants. There sat in varied motives the three other spectators: the ever-astounded Mrs. Jaramillo whose drawn-on eyebrows superseded her actual feelings almost on a 24/7-basis; the irascible Mr. Tijerina who wore his tension—all fifty years of it—on his shoulders; and the inarticulate Luis Ruiz who had just spent his second week in the States under the careful eye of Quintanilla and his family. The latter character sat at the bar, the other two at separate tables a sizable distance away from each other.

Now, before we can begin this episode proper, there are a certain number of items a spectator must know about our character before we move any further.

For instance, Old Crow had spent his former life out of Tiempo, traveling around the world on his writing. Magazines paid him to report, or engage in conversations, with various figures around the global map. "I love to pierce the spectator's shroud," Crow wrote of himself in the autobiographical note in the magazine for which he worked. "For me, writing becomes a vehicle for conversations." Never missed a chance to "conversate," as it were. He went to college in his youth seeking it; and when he had found it, he would write it down, not verbatim, but he was sure to get as much of it as he could remember. He would write his first novel on legal pads, ideas strung together by conversations. When it went by rather unnoticed, he turned to journalism as a way to obtain a livelihood for the thing he cherished most. "The written word," he has expressed in dust jacket blurbs, "is secondary to the spoken word. I come from an oral tradition."

"Perhaps in this way," Old Crow would further explain to fellow writers, alternatively in bars, coffee shops, and colleges, "I find some kinship to the Christian existentialists of the twentieth century. There is a distrust of the written word. And it *is* a spiritual conflict—but not in the way that it takes away from some god. No, my religion has long since set a millennia ago. I'm saying in the way that the written word is… well, it's in the phrase. It abstracts us from the deed, the doing. What good are printed words to the *existence* of life? That, and my people—some have come to understand this only recently—but my people are correct in distrusting a medium in which our deep and perpetual loss is etched into the annals of history. Those words aren't exactly charitable, now are they?"

He carried this reasoning with him everywhere he traveled, finding sympathetic ears, the nodding smiles, in the secret, intimate liberal meetings tucked away into the crevasses of consciousness. His interlocutors gazed upon his open face, long and rigid with thought, running parallel to his hair the same color as a crow's feathers. Child of the toasted maize.

The guarded face lifted in surprise when confronted with the eloquence with which Old Crow spoke. Something didn't add up.

A more cutting response, however, typically asked by the more discerning listener: "Why writer?" To which Old Crow would reel back and ponder. His mind wandered the parameters of his brain for the answer over the course of several decades, well into retirement age.

You could say that it was Xochi who convinced Old Crow to return to Tiempo, finally. Another one of their mutual friends informed him of her passing. He was staying at a cramped little hotel in New York when he received the call. The memories came flooding back. Memories of sweet citrus bursting in the mouth. How father used to sing on his way to work, dropping off your siblings. The slow eddy of wind across the palms. Sleeping in the school gymnasium during the big flood. Wincing at your first-grade teacher snoring all hell out of their nose. Spanish laying mute under a desk while English sashayed across spelling examinations. Climbing your first mesquite, slicing your palm open. Mom like a sun dial within and around the house.

Old Crow would move through these memories with working fingers, over decades out on the beat. Every time he received a postcard from Xochi, his mind would travel back over thousands of miles and a fistful of years. It was her death that mobilized his longing for return.

| * |

It wasn't until recently that the old man began to speak to what some people labeled as ghosts. Almost every night, one could find Old Crow at the Worm introducing invisible guests of his to random bar-goers. "I would love to introduce to you the prince of Xanadu. He just got off his private jet and is planning to spend some of his fortunes here." "Why, if it isn't the first lady president of these here States!

How's America from that big house?" "Don't tell me you haven't heard of this great person! They recently swam a great deal to get here—transatlantic!"

This is where we pick-up on our character, on a specific evening of early December, inside the smoky, dimly lit interior of the Tequila Worm. It proved to be an unusual year of weather in the Lower Rio Grande Valley, so the personality proclaimed on the flatscreen mounted above the bar. While national heat averages were high—and make no mistake, the Valley felt it doubly, as local weatherpersons opted for pastel-colored shorts to accompany their ironed shirts and ties—throughout any season not named *winter*, a front like a great reaching ghost stretched its curtain-like arms from the north and into the unsuspecting—or, rather, unprepared—South, rattling and overburdening power grids across multiple Texas counties. The caption crawl read—because the television was muted—"STOCK UP ON YOUR NON PERISHABLES KEEP YOUR PETS INDOORS CHECK ON YOUR NEIGHBORS." There was a stir among the bodies in the orange light of the bar's interior, but no eye followed the news above.

Instead, the audience of four, accustomed to one or two of the old man's inventions, stared in awe at the wrinkled figure sashaying round the place in his disheveled clothing and whipping gray ponytail. Old Crow's stone cheeks were now rosy, his eyes warm and inviting.

At first, Mr. Tijerina thought, 'Oh boy, this cuckoo again.' However, when Old Crow informed him of some lady's admiration toward him, Mr. Tijerina lowered his shoulders a decimeter and was at a loss. Who could have possibly found the old widow admirable? He huffed into his open paw and stroked his five hairs back over the spotted shiny scalp.

Mrs. Jaramillo, her drawn-on sharp eyebrows above where the natural ones could be, seemed taken by the old man's performance and clapped. She shouted to Quintanilla who averted his attention to her applause, "Sounds fun!"

The young Luis Ruiz, who truly couldn't comprehend what went on, sat and clapped, too, mimicking what he thought was right, intimating toward Quintanilla in Spanish, "I have no idea what is going on, but the noise is entertaining."

"Poor guy," Quintanilla told his nephew. "I don't even think he's from here. At least I don't remember him."

| * |

As he drove on home in the whirring night, Old Crow received a feverish impulse to write and, once home, rushed to the den for pad and pen.

When he reached for the idea, however, voices abruptly impeded him as his inventions intended to visit—only this time, the old man would notice, they were not inventions, but memories of people he met before somewhere in time, their manifestation each a spiraling fog: bodies, faces, mouths, eyes. They came one by one, in ethereal single-file, speaking to him. And he was neither terribly bewildered nor perfectly sane that he sat with intrigue listening to them.

There, Old Crow had ghostwritten many tales of many truths, and none of them the same; and once the faces and hearts left him, he began to write a prologue:

"This I know is true. That many a man and many a woman, since the dawn of our conception, have identified and defined an infinitesimal amount of truth. What proceeds is a spirit log, if you will, of the manifold souls I have had the pleasure to meet and know throughout the course of this body's lifetime. With these souls comes the opportunity for us to examine another life outside of ourselves, so that we may perhaps forget this reality, if only for a second—forget that the clock keeps our beautiful error of humanity in its slender hands. Prepare to be surprised, and don't forget to listen to the sounds of the ghosts that exist as exhales of heavy souls both dead and alive.

"Now, of the voices that proceed and the truths attached to them: Not one person can judge them effectively. I try to prohibit myself from it. I cannot say whether they are ugly or beautiful. I can only give them a platform…"

Old Crow would find no extrication from writing until the following morning. Whether or not he would publish the work that had so urged him to finish went to the old man. 'Who would want to read the ramblings of an old crow like me?' he wondered. And at that point, he considered the word 'crazy.' For some reason, he allowed its passage into his mind, examined it, felt it. And for the first time, he was able to see himself outside of himself and thought of his writing, the voices, his mind. He conceived of the possibility that the voices and his mind were one. Perhaps he had gone crazy. Perhaps the people he talked to were an invention of the mind, perhaps a ruse even. The more he thought about it, the more reality seemed lacking. It seemed hollow. It seemed cold.

He thought he saw his ghost slip out of his mouth.

He forgot to turn on the heater last night. The cold of winter whispered into the home through the cracks of the windows—and he didn't remember if he had left one open earlier the previous night or in the daytime, thinking, 'You old fool,' but saying, "You're always leaving windows open."

He lifted himself from his deep swivel chair and donned an austere disposition, the face he wore hollow but manifested by a mental urge, as if his mind quickly pulled on a mask.

His eyes gently rolled over Xochi's shelves, the stacks inching closer to him.

The chill tightened his joints.

"You're always leaving windows open," he repeated, merely to create noise in the lived-in house. His stiffening legs keeping a hurried pace, Old Crow investigated all of the house's windows. His eyes rolled over the rooms of the house while securing each window. His brows began to sink in a sweat of confusion. "Whose home is this?" he began to question, falling into the deep swivel chair. All windows were closed since the last red heatstroke of autumn.

He raised his hands stiff with cold; they smothered his face until he could no longer see the paintings and photographs and books and the long absence. "She was my best friend," he said into his marble palms like a pit. "They were all my best friends. And I miss them all." He stayed so as a golden sun broke into a sealed window. He thought, 'Ghosts,' and said, "You're always leaving windows open." He began to laugh, but he wouldn't know what he laughed for; or perhaps he laughed at everything: the ghosts, the cold, the windows, himself.

After his spell of laughter, tears began to roll down his pruned cheeks, caught by the crease of his smile.

'You old fool.'

Rapping at the window. Days had passed since the great northern ghost rolled blackouts all across Texas and threw its arms over Tiempo, saying, "This is mine." Reports of the elderly found still in their homes permeated whatever pockets of media available in the region. The slumber of winter was a uniform blanket in the sky, gray and billowy. Sparse buzzing generators. Residents sleeping in cars at the pump, metal rattling. The no-light, itself, a sound audible, like the great ghost sprawling in one great bedroom sigh.

Voices outside the house crept among the rattling and snapping of petrified and petrifying foliage. A face peers through a cloudy window. A young mustache, wide nose, searching eyes that scanned what contents were behind a layer of frost. "Do you think anyone is in here?" someone asks in Spanish.

"I thought your uncle said he lived here," the face at the

window answers in English. "We have to check just in case. Fuck, my breath is fogging up the glass…" Eyes discern a figure slumped over a desk in a chair. There was a terrible stillness in the house that did not rise. The hunched back of the figure did not rise with breath.

Two young men entered the house through an unlocked door to find an old man whose face was now soaked with his own drool. One hand hesitated but grasped the old man's shoulder, rocked him gently until the seemingly inanimate body convulsed, the eyes rolled, irises darting. "He's *restarting*," one voice said.

"Excuse me, sir," the one rocking the old man said, not too loud so as not to cause alarm. "My name is Tyler. Sorry for slipping in like this, but my friend and I—that's my friend Luis—we were concerned—you didn't look like you were breathing. We've been going all through the neighborhood—"

The wrinkled face smarted. He heard a rummaging in the room and turned to see one of the guys perusing the books surrounding them. His vision pushed past the two people in the room to the contents of the room itself. Sweat began to accumulate in tiny dykes in the furrows of his brow.

"Who am I?" the old man asked.

The one gazed at the other who stopped flipping through a book. The one holding the book, Luis, placed the book flush on the desk and began inspecting items strewn about the cool mahogany that, by this point of the day after a few nights of intense chill, sponged most of the overnight precipitation.

"They used to call me Coyotl," the old man said. He rested his head on the palm of his hand, staring downward at the open faces of the desk and the book that interested Luis moments ago. He stayed like that while the other two exchanged low talk about the next steps.

From his periphery a miniscule shine traveled across the desk with the effect of a barreling star cutting through a gelatinous sky. The twinkling was his drool, some of which had crusted-over on his chin, but most of which accumulated in a pool the size of a face. Ambitious molecules of the substance began to inch away from the whole, following a natural slope left by the curvature of the desk, snailing that much closer to the book splayed before him.

The old man lifted the book from its soggy demise, gazed upon it with newborn eyes, and flipped through the pages, some of which threatened to scram under a precarious hand. Luis and Tyler watched as the old man mouthed words to himself as if off in the distance a version of himself read them aloud, off in the distance of time and space, at a fixed point only he could travel to.

The old man began to laugh, seemingly at the contents of what he read. Luis gave Tyler a sidelong glance and said, "I'm telling you, my uncle said this guy's lost it. He keeps seeing these things no one can. He already forgot that we're here."

"Oh, Xochi," Coyotl said, still enraptured by the book.

"What was that, sir?" Tyler asked.

He placed the book on his lap and made to rise from the swivel chair. Luis availed himself to his side, holding Coyotl by the underarm. Once up, he began going throughout the house, listing items of significance to him. "... And here's a pocket watch her grandfather stole from a rinche—at least that's what she told us. It's stopped. And here's the plaque they gave us commemorating her death"—the motor of his lungs steamed through the thin lips, the eyes downcast again, but mixed with the fervor of rushing through the objects of the house—"Xochi was shot through the head, just minding her business. She wasn't demonstrating, like the others. But the police were getting so rough those days. She was just minding her own business. They showed us the trajectory of the bullet. Like the particle beam that cleared that Russian's skull. Poor Xochi. That's why they all left. But that's why I returned."

"I'm telling you, bro," Luis told Tyler. "He could be making all this up. We're wasting our time. He needs a doctor or something."

"Who are you talking about, sir?"

Old Crow turned to the two boys and like a curator announced to them, "Why, Xochi, of course! This is her mausoleum, and I am its keeper!"

The pair looked at each other disconcertedly.

"Are you okay, pa?" Luis asked. He leaned close to the old man.

"Perfectly fine! You see, I was just writing this manuscript. Now if you two don't mind, it's time to mend an old man's wounds."

Old Crow returned his attention to the desk and began to scribble more.

"I'll bring them back, and I'll bring them to you. My friends—they will stand up! I'll bring them back to you."

Through uneasy eyes, Tyler suggested from behind the dauntless old man, "I think we should take you out of here to someplace that has electricity, someplace warm."

The space about the house rushed through Old Crow's nostrils. There was a trace of the cosmos in the scent. Perhaps he imbibed the realm of the fleshless, too. It was a healing breath.

CHEATED:
DR. JEFFERIES RELATES THE NEWS

"It's about time you paid 26 a visit, doc."

"Alright, Gabby. Tell him I'll be right over. Just gotta look over his charts again."

"They tell you anything good?"

"It's… It's not good no matter how anyone sees it. I know the man's in a great deal of pain. Things can only get worse, it seems…"

"Doc?"

"I'll be right there. Don't tell him anything. *I* have to be the one. Who knows, maybe something will make sense by the time I get there."

"What are you doodling there, doc?"

"Oh, *this*?" I lifted my hand holding a red pen to reveal that I had been drawing a hat. "I've been thinking about a book I haven't read in quite a long time, I reckon. Ever had to read *The Catcher in the Rye*?"

She tries to perk-up by giving me the smile of an actress, some facial maneuvers but nothing going on backstage.

"I think they made us read it back in high school."

"Which must've been, what, a year ago?" I laugh but she doesn't get the joke. "Gabby?"

"*Yes*, Dr. Jefferies?"

"You know my burden of memory's on you: All these patients, all of them stacking up—the only way I've been able to keep up is because of you and your reminders."

('burden of memory?')

She smiles awkwardly and retreats into the hallway. The hallway light falling onto her face makes it seem like there's a mask slipping onto her face.

I've tried to be the good guy. To be someone that everyone at least respects. Realistically, it's impossible—especially in my position. People always say, Oh, it's hard to find a caring doctor. And I sympathize with them. I mean, some of my buddies over at other hospitals tell me these stories where they simply have to limit their job. A simple check-up, nothing too alarming, care to take this, here's-the-check procedure. Make sure you have your payment ready at the cashier window. There are a few specific reasons as to why they don't trust us, and that's certainly one of them: Our hand's always out, and boy is it a doozy of a hand. Big because it's always expecting. Slick enough to slide into the pockets of your life and take *something*. They think that we see them as a paycheck. And how can that be true if hardly any of them *pays*? And how can that be true if what we do is make their lives better? Theoretically. How much is a life worth? No one should have to answer that question, I reckon. It's a tough question. It's tough work—especially if you're the one to break the horrible news to someone—especially the terminal. From there I reckon there's a few options for them, as I see it. As I've *seen* it. They either undergo further treatment that just stacks even more on them. Then in the middle of it they have this look on them that says, Was this even worth it? Or they just decide to return to whatever life they're currently leading, only now with the burden of living heavier. They're scared, is what it is. Scared of that steep decline into darkness. That dark pool without edges. And it makes a body reconsider slightly about relaying that information. That not only are you going to die, but you are dying now at an accelerated rate. But it comes out. It has to. English, Spanish. It comes out.

My relatives always tell me, especially the ones on her side, A hospital is a place where people come to die.

It wasn't built for that. At least I don't reckon so. I remember when I first got here, and this building was only a few stories tall; and the only thing you could really see for miles was that bank over in

McAllen. (I think it's downtown now.) I didn't know how long I was going to stay down here. The folks told me that leaving Oregon would be a mistake; that marrying young and moving for love and adventure would only make me poor; that casting the anchor of my father's savings in the Deep South wouldn't pay off; that just because I liked "one of them" didn't mean I'd like "the whole lot of them." "It'd be one thing if you were one of them and she'd have been *our* daughter"—oh, dad.

The Spanish doesn't really bother me as much as it did. (Boy was it a problem.) It's easy to pick-up a new language when you're immersed in the culture, when most of your clients at the beginning of your career are from those *barrios*. Mostly grandmas and grandpas who may or may not have their son or daughter translating for them, while their kids just sit in the lobby working their phone.

The people are okay, too, although I will admit that something here is shifting. Not a lot seem to notice it, but there's been a decline of care for the elderly. You can see it in these kids. All these kids that spent their time complaining about every little thing suddenly have no time for the ones that raised them. They're taking the lead from the Anglos, wheeling their elderly into homes. Some old people don't want to stay with them anyway; don't want to stay with a generation that half-listen to them, eyes glued to some screen. I mean, I know I have it somewhat easy. My parents live all the way up in Oregon with Ed having really no choice but to take them on as his responsibility. (Ed's always had something like the Catholic guilt in him without ever uttering a single prayer his entire adult life.) But in an area where the elderly were the responsibility of the kids, it's moving a bit forward. It's as if there's no time for that anymore. I wouldn't have raised April like that. Would've put some regard in her had she lived to see an old age; hell, had she lived to see an age past a day she wouldn't live past us.

Do I still blame her?

I can't seem to let it go all these years after. My Victoria. It wasn't her fault we couldn't have kids. Couldn't. Whose fault can it be? I shouted to God until there was no voice left.

I can't go a goddamn five minutes without thinking about her. (Where's that napkin?) I'm not mad at you. (I thought I saw one somewhere on my desk.) I could never be mad at you. I miss you. I miss the way your hair smells out of the shower and the way you smile at me whenever I do something incredibly stupid the way your body feels at night the way you'd sing to me back when we were younger the way you probably don't think of me when you ride out You love riding them but now you can't. Now I'm afraid you can never do that.

"Where's that *goddamn* napkin?"

That's no way to think now, especially with my business right in front of me. She's not supposed to be my business. She's Mata's business. Good business he's doing on me. I see his face everywhere now, always underneath a surgical mask, only his eyes burrowing into me deep. I hate everything about those eyes. I hate the way his eyebrows loom over them, always stern, always about to report bad news. I hate the collection of folds underneath the lids and how his tiny moles peek out for air. Who does he think prescribed his wife with downers when she started getting menopause—a favor for both of them? And when he was first shadowing me as some annoying thirty-something years ago, who was the guy that promised and made sure he got a job after his schooling was finally over? He would be *nowhere*—

And then Rachel coming in to stir the pot. I bet she enjoyed doing that to me; she found some sick sense of justice behind that painted face. As if the body of what I had done was turned inside-out in front of me—

But that's not what's important right now. What's important is… Mr. Felix Maldonado. (There's a little stain on this. Maybe coffee.) Good man. Someone reminded me Felix works—or *worked*—for our mailroom downstairs. I wasn't his *friend*, really, but sometimes when we'd bump into each other when I passed the mailroom, I would say hello and give my regards to his wife and son. I wasn't aware when he had taken off some days from work. (Apparently the man never took one day off. Saved his vacation days. I wouldn't doubt that he barely started using them *now*.) So, when he came to me in uniform one afternoon giving me vague symptoms, I had forgotten his name. I wasn't completely to blame—that was during the time I put all my money on Mata to pull-through for *me* once and for all. And so I told him that a beer helped whatever it was that ailed him.

Now, what's the matter with this guy? What's the matter?

Oh wait, now I remember. What's the matter is I can't understand the problem with him. His chart's all over the damn place. Poor bastard. Says he's been to about five other doctors before me; and it's no wonder since the first time I went to see him, he told me everything he thought was wrong like he was reading off a script. That's when you know they're thinking, This asshole better be the *best* asshole—better than any other asshole I've met. Well, I'd hate to be just another asshole, because this just doesn't make sense—*and* his ultrasound worries me. There's a mass sitting quite comfortably there, an ulcer no doubt.

Dammit.

Why can't this make any sense? I know I'm not trying hard enough.

I remember going to a mental health seminar some years ago. This was one of the symptoms of a catalog of psychological illnesses: being scattered. Scattered, fragmented, whatever you want to call it. One of those young doctors would certainly have diagnosed me with some form of depression, I reckon. That's all still kind of vague for me. It's another escape for people. Get 'depressed' and some pills, and you've got an entire generation high and careless. That's what this is all about; they don't like communicating to the outside world that they have to invent an internal problem to shrink away from it. They're just deceiving themselves.

—And if we move to the next slide, we can totally see, like, the

laundry list of symptoms. And yes, the bullet points are frowny faces.

- *feeling despondent, ignored, jettisoned from a world that does not care you exist*

- *negative behavior, such as being such a downer at a party, or sitting with a group of besties and moping for no apparent reason*

- *irresponsible choices, such as playing videogames for an entire evening, or taking up a dangerous hobby without letting your spouse know—(how dare you)—or getting touchy-feely with a nurse over whom you impose your esteem and authority in the clinic five years ago, thus jeopardizing their career*

- *identifying with "millennials" and their swaths of "emo" bands like that terrible Nirvana—(if you can call that music haha)*

- *living and wanting it to be over*

- *scatterbrained, or an unwillingness to stay on-topic, like ignoring the complete violation of a colleague by fawning over classic literature*

- *using the internet for activities other than emailing and researching*

- *easily offended by remarks/jokes*

—If you have any one of these symptoms, or find yourself in the middle of one of these clauses, chances are: YOU'RE DEPRESSED. High fives all around! That concludes—

No, no. Depressed is being a hysterical woman, like Maude, but you translate that to soft men, always showing and telling their sadness. My father never felt "depressed." Even if he did, he'd die before letting it show. You pack it in. You busy yourself. You watch a film. Go for a walk. Fuck. Read a book. For Chrissake, *do* something…

That damn Holden keeps coming to mind. Must have reread that book just about twenty times now. Used to love that scene of him watching his kid sister riding that carousel over and over again. I remember reading it for class in high school, and Mr. Palomin asked us to analyze that scene. I couldn't think of anything but how nice Holden made it sound.

I see it differently now.

You know what? I don't think it would hurt to visit her. I really think it wouldn't. I'll just take, um, Maldonado's papers with me. Now how many patients is that? Think I've had about four already. The numbers creep up. They stack and stack until you've got all these bodies with no names.

Wait a minute. Rachel must be looming nearby, I reckon. She may not be in the room, but I know she's around, lurking the halls, behind a desk. I know she's watching for me. I don't know why, but I can sense it from her. Hell, she was the one that told me what I already knew *what I already knew She stood there in front of her* She whispers it to me. She fucking whispers it to me, like she could hear her, for Chrissake, like she could hear her. She could shout it to me, and it wouldn't wake her up. Not from that sleep. I don't say anything to her. What right does she have to repeat those words back to me, standing there like some sort of statue about to come to life, repeating thoughts to me that have already taken many turns boiling at the back of my skull? She put her hand on my shoulder. I don't say anything to her. I don't ask for forgiveness or her mercy. She's reduced me to nothing. I look into her face, and her eyes are avoiding me. I know she wishes I were the one in the hospital bed, partly crushed, the hands that were used to violate her inanimate, tensed and frozen. Her hand felt like fire burning away, melting my shoulder, until she quit the room.

I go to her. I go to her bedside. I go to her bedside and take her hand like this, not exactly like when I took it when the horse fell on you—yeah, you. You can't hear my thoughts, can you? You used to say that you could read my mind, been reading it since the day we met; and I never understood that. I think the closest I got was when it fell on you. I knew something was wrong after I started heading back to your dad's old house outside Tiempo. I don't know how I felt it, but it came like god's hand gripping my consciousness through the vortex. Should I have loved you more? Should I have told you to stop riding those damn horses after the first time you fell from one? I know I couldn't't've. It's dangerous, but one look at you on one—with one hand invisible under the mane, and the other gripping the saddle— meant more to me than any faith I could impose myself in. In a way, I'm jealous that you had something like that

You would ride from the afternoon to the evening time, just around the fencing or out into the brushlands And the times of day as the sun went down would show on you and the horse the way tea shows on water And you would ride out, sometimes at a trot, sometimes at a brisk peel through sunflower crops with no petals Your short hair, what little it was since you always had it short, lifted into the wind as did the smile onto your face You'd ride off into the sunset like one of those old westerns where the good guys always win Outlaws, you told me They're called outlaws And I smiled to you and said Do you consider yourself an outlaw but you smiled and kept on riding on past me into the setting sun, you and the horse And as the two of you rode on further away from me, the harder it was for me to distinguish either of you until you came back in

It just took one day for it to happen Hell, it probably took but a couple of seconds, I reckon.

Now, I can't go. I can't go. All of this thinking, and now I don't feel like going.

I just need to get back to what's at hand; and what's at hand… is my patient. Fifth patient today. (There goes another doctor into surgery.) It doesn't even feel like I've been walking anywhere but in place; and it's a good thing Rachel entered my head; otherwise, I would've been there right now having a crappier day.

—U R D-Pressed—There, the title of this slide says it, haha.

No. I'm not. You want to pack this shitshow away now?

Of course, you're depressed. Look at how you're dressed!

Look at your life, man! Adulterous. Villainous. Your wife probably one stirrup in the grave. You need to see the next slide. It has a miniature horse as the background!

My wife is fine. She's going to wake up.

Face it, man. She's gone! And what will be left for you?

She can't be gone, she's still here! She's still breathing!

Denial is a symptom… Wait, don't walk away from the mic! Where are you going—

And there's his room.

What the hell am I going to say? I don't even have to go in. But Gabby came in and told me that he's expecting a visit. Christ, a month in here, and I'm surprised he hasn't let me have it. I know I would. I felt like hitting Rachel that day—*As if laying hands on her once wasn't enough Is that why you took up horses because you had to busy yourself knowing I had done something unforgivable* And because of what I already know

"Hello, Mr.—um—Maldonado…"

we can't And that GODDAMN Rachel

"I've been looking at your charts, and…"

the two of you rode further away until you couldn't come back

"And I don't think you're going to make it."

THE MIRROR
PART 1: A FAMILY AFFAIR

She had remembered what she told her grandson when he was a boy, a year or so before he could claim nothing between them but chance encounters and familiarity. He had asked her what *brujas* were.

"Witches," she answered, her leer cold and haunting yet untargeted. "Women that practice witchcraft." Her thin lips did not hunt for the words; the words flowed past from non-thought, as is the custom of those who hold reservations. When she had answered his question, she felt the stillness in her son's house as she held onto her grandson's hand, circling his knuckle with her thumb. Off in another room a radio wedged underneath a window sash buzzed with static, perhaps a broadcast of the sound of the waves perpetually crashing at the island. She listlessly stared off into an adjoining hallway, straight at a china cabinet, half expecting someone, even the shadow of someone, to cross before it.

"Are you a *bruja*, *'buela*?"

She raised her head and cackled like one would. She answered in question: "Who said that about me?" Aware of the rapport among the people with whom she has come into contact, any name or list of names wouldn't surprise her.

Particularly, she had never liked her cousin Ernesta; in fact, Araceli had hated her for most of their lives living together in both her parent's home and the home she helped build with her husband Florencio, back in the early sixties, when her father granted money to his only beloved daughter for such a purpose. Araceli Lucio disliked Ernesta since they were children, and she knew her cousin reciprocated the sentiment, the evidence of which not only manifested in petulant expressions, but also in a single crime. Ernesta had stolen Araceli's hand mirror when they were both eight years old. The mirror, given to her by Leocadia, her mother, had completely captivated Araceli. She would take it everywhere, catching light and sending beams at different objects like a tiny searchlight, watching the circle of light change in shape and size across various terrain. It took the curve of her mother's cheek, bit into the shadow of her father's boots, became nothing when cast off into the open day. She would mostly direct beams at any darkness, at night laying it beneath her window on a slant to reflect the moonlight into her otherwise moonless room. Noticing how her daughter utilized the object in a manner contrary to its popular use, Leocadia told her that as long as she had the mirror she would have light, that looking into the mirror she would see herself always, even in total darkness; that to look into it was to acknowledge yourself, knowing that there's you and there's you again in a way you've never seen before; and when Araceli did peer into it in darkness, initially she saw nothing, but then she would piece together images of what she looked like until she would see the round of her face in a bluish hue that darkness yields to the seeker; and there she would sleep knowing that she existed as sapphire.

Her mother's gift did not relent in its utility, for when Araceli inexplicably caught fever soon after, the mirror would provide her with friends. Sometime during these waves of heat, she would stop writhing in her bed momentarily. Outside she heard the oncoming sound of a march, non-uniform and easy; the sound of the creaking well reel lightly splashing bottom; her mother's soft voice. The mirror peeked outside through a break in the dark curtain and relayed images of white-clothed entities gently beat by sharp sunshine, decades of it. Unable to blink, she cried sweltered tears that mixed with sweat. The mirror had cut through the lonely days of fever and brought her ghosts under sombreros, the fraying straw puncturing the sun.

Nearly two months later, she would recall this serene instant amidst her suffering when Ernesta stole the hand mirror from her during play. She knew that Ernesta would watch her play with the mirror. Araceli constantly angled the reflection of light into Ernesta's eyes, blinding her for seconds until the light became a flashing point in her vision that melted in color. Araceli would also catch Ernesta spying on her when gazing into it. There Ernesta was straddling a branch, peeking around a corner of the house, stealing peripheral glances while she pretended to color.

She wouldn't know it at that time, but Araceli received an explanation from her cousin that day. Araceli confronted her with an unflagging anger, her child's body making no physical advance:

"Tell me why you stole it."

Ernesta narrowed her eyes, her virulence lost on her but ever real to her cousin. She shouted to Araceli, "Because I cannot see them. Because I cannot remember them. Because you have what I cannot see or remember." Moments later, Araceli's father had to separate the two from toiling with each other in the stirring dirt.

"Now why are you two fighting?" Fernando asked, bracing their wrists with his hands. "I expect this behavior from other kids, not the two I've raised."

Ernesta turned to him with a defeated countenance.

"Why do *you* have to raise me?" Her arm hung in her uncle's grasp. "I didn't ask you to." She had let it enter the transmittable airspace in feverish breath, the meaning of which shrouded her cousin's head with resentment, the feeling of which would echo, become infinitesimal, mistaken as interior monologue in lapses of sanity and memory, then and for decades to come.

And for those decades, Araceli lost the sense of sapphire she had gained from her magic tool. Instead, she would spend dark nights in dark meditation, limiting the interminable, electrical nimbus that is her mind to walls of darkness, deceptively profound and boundless.

| * |

It came to no surprise to her when her father, Fernando, stipulated that with the donation of constructing the house in which she and her husband would live that Araceli was to house her cousin. Araceli always knew her father to be charitable, even at the expense of his family's comfort. For Ernesta, specifically, her father seemed to upturn his own family if only for the chance of a modicum of his niece's comfort.

Both of the girls had just turned eighteen, and because other girls in school had begun to outwardly daydream of their wedding days—(rumors had gone around that Cynthia Escobar went absent for two weeks with the nausea of motherhood, deduced by Melissa Rangel who had done the same thing a year before)—the playful imagining of spouses elicited foresights of love. Ernesta held no prospects of finding a husband. Spinsterhood didn't concern her at all, as it did many of her peers. It wasn't because she wasn't attractive. On the contrary, men would outwardly pine for the stout girl throughout her adolescence, her curves titillating for the eyes, her broad shoulders and wide jaw reminiscent of warrior dreams. She and her cousin looked drastically different from each other, Araceli's frame more petite, her face trim and set elegantly with high cheekbones. No one told Araceli she had "hips made for birth" like Ernesta.

Ernesta had received many offers for courtship when she completed high school, but all for naught, overwhelmingly due to Ernesta's genuine disinterest. She really didn't care for romantic relationships. While her peers fawned over prospects of marriage, Ernesta would roll her eyes and extricate herself from the vicinity.

Araceli, however, exercised her right to fall in love with a well-to-do farmhand. That's how Ernesta would figure it, rather. Her cousin's passage toward marriage never came to turmoil; behind her cousin's more than fair complexion, there was no numb retching of the subconscious. Araceli led the normal life with ease. For that reason, and the other of which spawned in the opaque mud of her mind, surfacing as the explanation she gave her cousin as to why she committed theft: for these things she disliked Araceli; and as her thoughts churned and time lapsed, her disliking turned into bitterness and indifference. It developed like a rot in the brain and only worsened when her uncle forced Araceli to house her. Not only did she hate charity and pity, she abhorred the thought of paying witness to her cousin's flourishing marriage and—soon enough—family. She would foresee adulthood trapped in the peripherals of those with which she lived, always an afterthought, always a being-smeared-and-amiss.

Prior to her cousin's marriage, Ernesta lived in the backyard shed of her aunt and uncle's house, a bed built for her after halving Araceli's wooden bed frame, creating two twins out of a queen-size. Fernando had emptied the shed of its tools and sparse farming equipment, although at times he would catch himself tossing a hammer or loose lumber through the door, afterwards thanking God his niece was out playing.

Ernesta adamantly refused to share space with her cousin. Perceiving this sense of resentment toward his daughter with absolute forgiveness and resolution, though uncertain in how to keep the two separate short of building Ernesta a house of her own, Fernando had promised her that once his daughter left the house to start her new life, Ernesta would quarter in her cousin's room. What Fernando didn't expect was that his brother Humberto, who he had not seen since Uncle Sam drafted him, would arrive in Tiempo sans mom or dad to come home to, since they had vacationed in Mexico and disappeared near the Sierra Madre Occidental mountain range during Humberto's deployment.

Humberto arrived decorated, "off the boat," as he would put it with what his brother would regard as a humbling smirk; for Fernando had never known Humberto to fully smile. But there he presented it, revealing teeth soaked in the juices of pockets and tins of chewing tobacco, at the doorway of Fernando's house, the evening sun high behind him. Fernando embraced him and offered to take his bags.

"If it is all the same to you, brother, I traveled all this way with this weight—what are a few more steps, eh?" Humberto said.

Always adhering to a penchant for adventure and discovery, Humberto had sought to leave the Lucio household the moment the opportunity presented itself. By the age in which the government drafted him to fight the Vietcong, forty years old, he had traveled to a few southern regions of Canada, settled for a few years in the wine country of Northern California, and returning to the Rio Grande Valley, served as a tour guide for investors seeking property to set up shop. Fernando would say to Leo when Humberto's name would come up after seeing Araceli and Ernesta to bed, the coffee thundering in the percolator, "I feel since he is older than me, and yet still unmarried, he tries to fill his life with these great wanderings." In the interim of the burgeoning of Fernando's household, Humberto had skirted the bubbling cauldron of love, amounting to a handful of instances with a number of women, almost all of whom resented the innateness of his wanderings; his need to pick-up-and-go left indelible marks on their brows, elicited spiteful lip curling where he had shyly bitten. Humberto obeyed his one true longing: movement. A sudden frill of excitement ribboned his smirk as Fernando had written him months before his dismissal, informing of their parents' disappearance; something about his parents *finally* venturing outside their home of thirty years, stationed adjacent Tiempo's first graveyard, children of the plow and soil—their misfortune filled him with an anxious joy, although he had difficulty discerning that anxiety, perhaps due to their fate of vanishment, whether they be alive or dead. Life and death in this situation melded into one. When the army had released him to rejoin "normal American life," he developed a strange confluence of living: The experience of life seemed to bust at the seams, for he would wake on a train headed south toward Texas, and he could have sworn the rattling, charging machinery, the wind pressing soft, kneading knuckles to the window on which he rested his head—he must have been about to drop onto foreign land, hand ready to pull the chute. He had become painfully aware of this temporal conflation. He started questioning reality and his place in it. At all times he was never sure whether he lived in the present or if he was simply stuck in a revisitation of the past. And so, when he rapped at his younger brother's door, he could not stifle the doubtful thoughts until he saw that familiar face, so similar to his that passersby confused them for twins when they were children, mostly due to Humberto's stunted growth.

He entered through the living room with long confident strides, the house opening itself up to him, lived-in, his brother undoubtedly spending his siesta time on the vinyl couch off to the side in what he assumed to be the living room, the slippers of a wife with naggingly cold feet resting before a glass coffee table of which the smell of glass cleaner, perhaps a blue liquid, clung in miniscule bursts of ammonia that could kill a roach if properly drenched. The whole house smelled of cleaning products and subtle ribbons of flowers. *Here* was a home. Because Humberto was interested in "setting camp," Fernando and Leocadia led him to their daughter's old room half devoid of any remnants of previous decoration. Araceli was a sparse enough girl growing up to live without much, save for a few toys, a jewelry box, clothing, and her mother's mirror. She left with mostly everything, except for her mirror, which had been stolen, and a scribbled map in blue marker on the wall to the left of the bed. Her parents had tried to scrub the marker off, but to no avail; and they couldn't figure out where the map led, if it led anywhere. The jagged boundaries reminded the adults of the Valley and Mexico and in the Southwest triangles that Leocadia thought were trees; and then some indirect scribbles leading to the triangles, the curving lines never once touching each other. It remained a family mystery for quite a while, a mystery even more inconclusive since the cartographer, Araceli, would draw blanks as to its origin and meaning, only divulging that she had drawn it during the fever that ravaged her.

At night, however, with the one light bulb swinging after a yank on the cord, Humberto would study the map in earnest, replicating it on a notepad. He laid on his niece's childhood bed holding the note to the light, tracing the lines with a finger. It seemed simple enough: a child's fevered scribble, possibly an outlet for the pain stored inside her. Nonetheless, he kept the note with him as he carried out his life with his brother and sister-in-law. Not one to be idle, Humberto found ways to keep busy. Before long he was heading into town on random construction jobs, the latest of which—craning into place a giant clock onto an old watchtower—would necessitate night-hands.

Before heading off to help with the future clocktower, during a late evening telling stories with the family circling a pit of smoldering mesquite outside in the last embers of evening, he held the note before the crackling fire. Translating the image over the waning glow transformed the mysterious items. No longer were the triangles trees: they revealed themselves to be mountains. The scribbles no longer snaked aimlessly around the paper canvas: it was one unbroken line weaving through the mountains, having a starting point and an end.

Fernando noticed his brother's complexion. And Humberto noticed this. He retrieved the note into a jean pocket.

Fernando nodded at him, to which Humberto replied, "Thinking of a story, Nando," his face illuminated in the orange grainy firelight. He always carried with him a repertoire of campfire stories, the majority of which were true. The true ones evaded him, as his reaching for them returned jagged, clipping memories that produced a frosty veil of sweat over his brow. He felt Leocadia, Florencio, and Araceli stare at him in expectation. Ernesta's shadow, outside the fire's minutely shifting perimeter, sat on the stump of the tree whose warmth the rest of the family imbibed.

The stillness of the night suffused the airspace. The liquid, limpid moon pierced through the darkness with white but shrouded Tiempo in blue so that way the city, the houses, the mesquite existed twice-over: they were things and their shadows in a world asleep.

Clouds in lapping hills of cotton fringed the palace of the moon.

Humberto told a story about a boy tramping through the Valley heading toward the coast. The boy awoke one day and found his parents missing. The boy searched throughout the west side of the Valley, obtaining meals from sympathetic adults, and sometimes shelter, but ultimately stealing into the twilight leaving no trace of his presence.

Having covered half of the Valley, the boy decided to head to the coast but got lost in Tiempo, in a *monte*. (No one had come by to call this area "Tiempo"; no one had settled it, nor drawn its limits.) In the *monte*, the sounds of buzzing, croaks, hisses, snaps, hoots, and the silence between everything engulfed him. Branches went every-which-way, pointing in contradictory directions, and there lingered a haze perpetually glistening in the foreign, sparse light. He had heard of *montes* before: his parents had always threatened to leave him stranded in one if he continued misbehaving. "Like parents sometimes think about doing, but at a market, or the bank"—Humberto said in an attempt to startle Araceli and Ernesta, both of whom surpassed the age these scares necessitated in order to be effective. 'You don't have kids yet,' he thought, continuing the story.

The boy couldn't find his way out after the first day. Layers upon layers of branches and wet tassels of leaves obscured his escape. The dizzying sounds of the *monte's* tiny percussion ensemble tricked him at every turn; when he thought he had sharpened his hearing enough to discern an absence of *monte* sounds, bounding over engorged roots, scraping his blanching skin on mesquite spikes, he would discover that what he had heard was not an opening, but another clearing. The second day passed by with the same results, only this time, he thought he heard his parents, his father about to admonish him, his mother in woeful compliance. On the third, the boy decided to stay put under a clearing and let his mind wander and saw the sun in static motion. He could see the sun for its yellow hue, and it reminded him of afternoons with his father who lost his patience the moment he stepped through the front door, making good use of the belt used to suspend his pants underneath his overbearing paunch, not to mention whacking his child—oh, the dreams the boy had of lassoing his father by the neck in his sleep; and his mother who witnessed everything and did nothing, wearing the complexion of absence, her attention turned away, toward the feminine duties of the time, enforced by a husband whose mania and violence burgeoned after the birth of his only son.

As the sun dipped minutely outside the dome of the sky-clearing, the boy came to entertain the possibility that his parents had abandoned him, like they had always threatened to do on multiple occasions. Then it occurred to him that he had aged two years since he began to search for them. He thought that he had traveled everywhere in the Valley, creating a mental map of every town, every dirt road, every person in relation to direction and place. He began laughing at the realization of getting lost in a single natural blemish, one dark crescent on his map.

He had gone days without substantially eating; and the days

evolved into years of fasting. He remained in the clearing, under the eye of the sky, "Breathing and mourning," Humberto said, making sure to punctuate his next phrases, "Breathing and crying. Breathing and smiling. Breathing and laughing.

"It is said that if you go to the *monte* in the north of Tiempo, you can see his body there, pickled with youth, with the breath of childhood sounding from the branches of his lungs." He let the story end there and stared into the fire.

Two stars twinkled among the billowy hills that had only become stretched-out and jagged by yawning winds.

His audience stared at him—Ernesta gazing somewhere else, possibly the stars—but the others stared at him.

PART 2: THE CURSE

No one had heard from Humberto after he left Fernando's house for the mountains of Mexico one year after he returned from Vietnam. Leocadia with a bare leg stemming out of a turquoise sheet, Fernando, face submerged in a naked pillow, balding arm draped over the outline of her ribcage, the sheer caramel drapes swelling by their twin-snoring; Araceli's lengthy curls splayed beyond the lumpy blanket spread and scrunched on the living room floor, Florencio with his head nestled in the cavity beneath her shoulder and the balls of his feet enduring the frigid linoleum, bedroom not too far away, house complete in structure but nearly devoid of furnishing; Ernesta staring into the dark window above her bed, starlight spilling out of its corners hour after hour: This was the status from which Humberto, lacing his boots tightly, departed without warning, without alarm or disruption, without leaving much of anything behind. He had only left a note on his bed, a sheet torn out of the notebook in which he scribbled examinations and theories, reading, "Thank you for everything. To Leo: Take care of Nando. For Nando: The search begins, but our blood will always connect us, like strands to *Aztlán*. Do you feel it?"

Humberto stole into the turning colors of twilight, advancing past the clocktower he had helped install, his own hands corrugated by the alignments of gears and the long iron hands like stitching needles weaving time. Although not as tall and bulky as the bank in McAllen, the Tiempo Clock lurked in the skyline periphery and seemed to follow and linger in his march toward Mexico…

Araceli would report to her parents that she was expecting. To the perfunctory eye, the newlyweds' commitment to sex must have been in service to this exact outcome. In Araceli's eye, she could hardly wait through the Catholic abstinence before finally peeling off the jeans of which contained a talisman of rapturous mystery. Florencio's tall, lanky stature, mirroring most of the Maldonado men, was an animate scarecrow pitching into the corn and cotton fields of his father.

His family owned land north of the Tiempo Basilica, some would say the nexus of the city, as nearly every citizen seemed to circulate through the sidewalks swept of dirt; through towering wooden doors forever open; through marble halls passing bowls of holy water, rows and rows of pews with wooden, sin-dilapidated kneelers, and portraits successively depicting the story of Jesus, the last of which led to the *Virgen* centerpiece, set high above the pulpit, her somber, humble outline carved in golden curls. To look at Mary from a pew invited one to falter in contemplation of the great Mystery. On the morning in which Araceli, from a hallway flanking the pews and the pulpit, first saw Florencio kneel with grave impetus before the Father issuing Communion, Mary's countenance seemed to her one of curiosity, of seeking satiety.

Araceli never took alarm in Florencio's lack of a high school education. He would assure her that farming would never cease in the Valley's economy, that his father would always have work for him, and that he would inherit whatever spoils his father accrued. The then-nineteen-year-old Araceli found safety in Florencio's postulations, made typically in his lean arms, the musk of bathwater and faint dirt and sweat eliciting her affection. During these sessions of closeness, Araceli would wrap her legs around one of Florencio's, her womanly warmth and dampness closing-in on his thigh. She felt a throbbing through two layers of jeans, neither one of them addressing their suppressed lust.

It was nearing her Tio Humberto's one-year anniversary staying in Tiempo—(and not for too long, as it were)—capping a week of post-wedding breakfast/lunch/dinner fucking, when it had happened on the blanketed bed of Florencio's truck underneath an open summer's night. Her mother prepped her before the honeymoon, letting her in on the secret of life and the gift that followed morning-after sickness, the latter detail Araceli fully realizing off the side of Florencio's Chevy in pink twilight. Between this factor and the first time Florencio entered her, the first time *anyone* entered her, she grew increasingly suspicious of her own body. Nonetheless, Florencio persistently made love to her, herself developing tiny theses about his own morality.

"I don't understand," she said to him after rediscovering each other's bodies once more out in his father's fields. "My whole life, when there is talk about the natural occurrences of women—what happens *to* us—there is always this avoidance. We become untouchable. Things left alone." She directed the rearview mirror toward her. The sunset provided an orange light that reddened creepingly. High sunflowers swayed with a chance breeze, creating a static noise suffusing the fields of budding cotton plants. "I'm breaking out, too."

Another hand appeared in the mirror, caressing her face. "I never understood," Florencio began, "how a body transforms and we can still be the same person. Like now: I see you"—he cups Araceli's cheeks with two palms—"and you say you are changing, yet you are still the woman I love. You are still the woman I saw staring at me at church that one day. That is the miracle, yes? How Jesus can be torn and all and we still receive Him like an everlasting love. That is how I see you." On the ride back home, with the stars overhead, he put a hand of long skeletal fingers over her stomach, no more use for words but a smile.

The news of Araceli's pregnancy came to the surprise of no one; however, Ernesta received it with stolidity, of which ushered her into a world of even worse enmity; enmity not only against her cousin, but also against herself and her unchangeable past. For not only would she witness the growth of her enemy's family, Ernesta would also retch with a phantom pain, except she, herself, was the missing limb without having ever belonged to a body. And the pain struck like a toothache that coursed through every cranial nerve, pulsating with a stabbing absence. The absence could not and did not diminish with the presence of Tio Fernando or Tia Leocadia. They had taken her in as a girl, but she grew to resent them as well.

The only time Ernesta felt a hint of familiarity was during the night Tio Humberto told his story of the boy in the *monte*. She felt that someone had tramped away with something of hers and that in the pit of her being there formed a *monte*, with the mesquite spikes poking into her and on the grounds never a certain step. What she never felt in her soul was the warmth of the sky clearing, the illumination amidst everything in effort to shun it.

Her Tio's disappearance filled her with a pulling sensation, of which coincided with her small joint business venture with her Tia Leo, knitting hats, scarves, and mittens at the latter half of winter, into spring, the true South Texas "winter." Leo had always busied herself while Fernando sold flower arrangements in the heart of Tiempo's business district. At times, she would avail herself to the demands of Fernando's shop, assisting not only with large floral arrangements, but also with the occasional wedding service, taking on the duties of stitching dresses meant for daughters not her own. The shop's business withered in wintertime, however. Counting the nights when the whole house smelled of burning propane from the kitchen, spying the glassy eye of her husband staring at the curtain off the side of the bed, Leo began knitting, heading into town during the workday to turn a profit, buying enough groceries that would not seem too conspicuous. She enlisted her niece in her plight, rewarding her with a cut of the sales. Ernesta would pocket the money and buy herself groceries that she would make the same day, or, more often than not, eat cheap bar food at the various *cantinas*, such as the Tequila Worm. This afforded her escape from the dinnertime quiet spent between herself and Araceli and Florencio. As the days advanced, the newly wedded couple saw very little of Ernesta, walking past her bedroom in their house without rapping on her door, for fear of disturbing what little peace suffused throughout the halls.

Ernesta, in fact, did not sleep under their roof. Although there was a designated room for her in Araceli's house, and a newly open room after Humberto's absence, every afternoon when Tia Leo would dismiss her from knitting, Ernesta would sneak into the shed of her childhood, resting on the familiar bed ripe with the sweet, musty smell of nostalgia in the plaid, rippling bedsheets, plucking sparse cords of thread that clung to her clothing.

Between the two, Ernesta and Leo manufactured winter wear with austere efficiency. Looping threads, cross stitching, finger-pricking. During the weaving, Ernesta never forgot her Tio Humberto's story; she saw it enacted in her threads; how one can get lost and erased in overlapping lines pulled tight over existence. The story demanded something from her. She knew where these sensations were endeavoring to lead her.

On a morning in which many of Tiempo's citizens turned their television sets and radios on to catch the broadcast of Pope John Paul II's visitation in Mexico City, Ernesta had made pilgrimage northward. It had taken her all morning and most of the afternoon to traverse the one long nameless caliche road that ended a yard before her destination. She stepped through tallgrass that tickled and irritated her ankles despite the long skirt that never stirred because there lacked any breeze or any hope for one. Pearls of sweat rolled down from her temples; the faint hairs on her arm matted by a heavy day's humidity.

It looked like a facade. She felt that if she blew, it would fall; and for this reason, the thought of venturing within slightly unnerved her. From behind her, however, she could hear the sound of an incoming wind that successively put her hair, skirt, and body into motion toward the *monte*.　She brought with her a spool of red yarn and tied an end to the first branch she met before proceeding any further. Her intuitiveness gave her a sense of satisfaction, yet another gust of wind that almost seemed like an inhale from the *monte's* jagged maw erased the smirk from her face; and in she almost fell, wordless.

Before she had lost all traces of the red sun, she produced a flashlight from the elastic of her skirt, turning it on while she glanced back at the overlapping arms of mesquites and the reds of the light of the sun and her yarn, the only indications that there was a world outside of the *monte*, that there was Tiempo.

Any trace of the sun vanished the further Ernesta explored the breath-sucking wood.

What she thought to be the hissing of a snake blanched her brown face, subsequently walking into a sheet of mosquitoes that tried their best to drill into her; and they would have, too, had Ernesta's incessant swatting not deterred them. While she fended off the miniature vampires, she felt the last of her yarn pluck the spool from between her fingers. She immediately went to the ground to search for the lifeline. The second Ernesta spotted the end of her red yarn, however, the snapping of twigs in close proximity split her mind from her body, the former ordering the stultified latter to escape. Her eyes locked onto the yarn, but her mind raced and wailed and jammed simultaneously.

| * |

When she arrived late that night walking the same nameless road, now purple from the distorted light of a hidden moon, Ernesta meandered from the crunching caliche under her feet to the calm reception of dew-licked grass whose near silence each step nauseated her. The house—that great mansion where she never existed as a whole—stood dauntless underneath a starless sky. Not a noise stirred from within the house, at once giving the effect of hollowness that wrung the wind of its languidness, yet built from its humidity a choking breath that entered Ernesta's nostrils but caught in her throat. The next instant, she vomited, the yet-borne memory reimaging in a mustard fog of what she had done.

"You can never take it back," called a voice from the faraway *monte*, and it was law. It echoed with distortion; she was unsure whether it was her own voice or…

She felt eyes giant and unblinking upon her, overcast in the sky.

She entered through the back entrance that led into the kitchen, allowing the screen door to clap back. The intimate sound of disrupted bedsheets and the suction-cupping of padding feet over linoleum. There in the dining room Araceli stood underneath a halo of light. The sight of her made Ernesta's veins jump, all in opposite directions, and she collapsed in the kitchen. She couldn't bear Araceli's eyes on her.

Araceli ran to her and rested her cousin's head on her lap. "You were gone for so long. Where have you been?"

Ernesta breathed heavily, attempting to expel the stinging miasma in her lungs. "I did it. I did it; and if you have ever found yourself in the middle of good and evil, what I have done now will make you truly hate me." Her eyes kept avoiding her cousin who eclipsed the dining room light.

Her words unnerved Araceli. "What have you done?"

Ernesta strained her head to keep her cousin's shadowed image away from her waking eyes, the veins taut against the skin of her neck. She felt Florencio's steps in the heartbeats caught in her throat. Her sight of the kitchen door began spiraling. Had her head rolled off from her body? She began to speak to abate the nausea:

"She spoke to me as if I was her child, Araceli. You must understand that. I *need* you to understand how she spoke to me. She called to me; she said, 'Come here, my pretty girl, *mi hija.*' She looked like an ancient woman, like she was a grandmother to a whole *barrio.* I knew who she was. I knew *what* she was. Her voice soothed me and drew me closer to her. I was entranced. Father de la Garza always told us how smooth the Devil talks! Her words invited me.

"'*Ay, que bonita.* Why don't you stay awhile?'

"I told her that I had to go, that I was lost. But she said that I was too big to be lost. Then we started talking. She kept asking for names. 'Where's your mom—who is she? Who is this boy you are looking for in this *monte*? Please stay awhile. Why are you sad?'

"I knew I should have left running, but she kept asking these questions. I couldn't see her right away. She was tall—the way her gray shawl hung on her made her look like a tentpole. She reached out with her hand, and underneath I saw she was naked. I saw the moonlight beneath her shawl. She kept moving closer and closer to me, but I didn't notice it until she almost held me and I could smell the fabric that smelled of mold and iron and animal. I still smell it on my skin. It's stuck to my skin"—she begins scraping her forearms, the dead skin in streaks of white shavings. Araceli braced her cousin's hands from tearing more flesh.

"Oh, but please don't make me stop. Let me pay with my skin, my Lord. *Dios*, she kept asking for *names* and why I was crying all of a sudden. That voice went into my conscience like a shucking knife. She began singing a song—that evil song: '*Duerme, duerme, negrito.*' I felt the tears hot on my cheeks. And that's when I heard it! A baby crying! Another voice in that dark *monte*! I didn't think it was possible for a baby to be in a place like that! I couldn't move when she went to a tree and picked something up from it. I couldn't see it too well at first, but I realized that it was the thing that made the crying noise. I barely saw any part of it, mostly its shadow. She was still singing when she raised the baby. '*Duerme, duerme, negritito.*' That's when I spoke your name—"

"What do you mean you *spoke* my name?" demanded Araceli, still clutching her cousin's wrists.

"I didn't mean to! I don't know if I was scared and only thought of screaming your name. But as soon as I said it, I knew something had shifted. Something had"—she began coughing—"My tongue! Why is my tongue swelling? I feel like—I want to swallow— my tongue!"

"What's going on with her, Araceli?" Florencio asked. The Maldonado family never bought into *brujerias*, and so he never knew what curses looked like. He didn't know what to make of these contortions, nor of Araceli's resolve.

"You finish telling me what you started," Araceli ordered Ernesta. She began shaking her, the throw of her cousin's spirit being pinched upward.

Florencio pressed a hand onto Araceli's shoulder. "We must take her to a doctor."

"I knew too late that naming you would ruin your life," Ernesta continued, her tongue returning to her with a bulbous flame. "At first, she wanted to take the boy away, but I pleaded with her—I pleaded and pleaded until she began to sing that song again. It reminded me of a trip I don't remember taking. *Mama, Mama*! There's the river! Can't we stop and watch!"

"Ernesta! Ernesta!" Araceli began lightly smacking Ernesta's face. "Come back to us!"

"Why aren't you looking at me, *Mama*? Did I say something wrong? Did I not call you *mama* when I first spoke? I take back my first word. I take it back. I said I take it back until my jaw hurt, but she did not change her mind. Then, I ran to her, Araceli, and I pushed her because I knew she was making something. The *molcajete* was dark and smelled of hell, Araceli. I almost threw up from the stench! Then the baby began to cry again, and it split my head. I thought it was my own hands that gripped my head—but it was her, holding it while she forced me to swallow that filth! She made me—" The nausea had bubbled up again.

"Please forgive me. Please forgive me. Oh, please forgive

me." Ernesta was on the verge of tears, and her voice grew hoarse and cracked like parched earth.

Araceli slid her lap from underneath Ernesta's head and stood over her. "I do not ever want to see you again." There was scarce venom in her words. Ernesta couldn't see her face. It was like looking into a mirror when the light is far away.

"Are you seriously believing this, Araceli?" Florencio asked. "*Brujeria* doesn't exist! What she has told you must be some big joke. She needs to see help."

"Before the sun rises," Araceli continued as Florencio helped Ernesta to her feet, "you shall be gone from my house. Do not ever return—even as a ghost." She turned away and walked to her bedroom, to what would surely be a sleepless and ceaseless night.

PART 3: THE WINDING END

She named him Felix. She and Florencio both fumbled for a name, for they hadn't thought about it at length. They named the baby after Florencio's uncle who had passed away before ever starting a family for himself. There had circulated a rumor amongst the Maldonado family that someone murdered Florencio's uncle, and that his uncle died a homosexual, the four corners of Texas vile and rough—almost as if by birth.

Baby Felix's infancy passed with ease, on a night where all windows were left open despite the superstition that demon dogs were perpetually on the prowl for newborns. After the doctor had left, however, Araceli felt the pulsing of Felix's heart through his fingers, contemplating how it seemed twice the meter of her own heartbeat. This gave her a slight cause for alarm. She wasn't sure whether Ernesta's warning held water or if it had been a farce; that perhaps her cousin hadn't really stopped the *bruja* from placing the would-be original curse on her and her baby. (She heeded curses. She was told on a few occasions about her great grandma Fela, on a bright day that betrayed no sense of safety crossing on foot from Reynosa to Harlingen, assailed with a full-body spasm, limbs tightening, joints jutting out of the skin until she was a box of a person suspended only by elbows and half a knee on the Anzaldua Bridge—*that* was no accident.) Her expression would slacken, and the uprightness of her spine would wilt as if an invisible god-hand suppressed her with cosmic law, when the child began eating dirt while playing in the orange groves next to the house. She could only surmise this behavior eliciting from the times they would visit Florencio's parents on their farm. Baby Felix gazed wide-eyed at the laborers plucking onions from the fields. He would reach out and babble at the baskets bobbing with golden unearthed orbs. Maybe if he dug into the land himself, he could find gold, too. The effect alone was cause for concern. Could this be the start of the end? Baby Felix would spend most of his baby time indoors, a measure that Araceli saw curve his fixation with dirt.

At the age of seven, now with the ability to form words before and after telling them, Felix would begin to socialize with some children from a neighboring house down the road perpetually about-to-be-paved. ("Caliche will be a thing of the past," Tiempo's then-

Department of Transportation Head, Eric Ericson, was reported saying. Eric Ericson: forever filling-in inner-city potholes.) Orange cones punctuated the caliche road leading north. Although he had quit eating from the earth, Felix realized the taste of dirt had returned to his palette after he spotted a shadowy figure at the end of the baking road. He would be in the middle of tag when he swore that he could pick little clumps of dirt from the pockets of his teeth with his tongue; and it beckoned him to look around, but it was always the same place where his eyes met with the shadow: It would stand before a background of mesquites surrounded by beige nothing. (While tax money funded inner Tiempo construction projects, leagues of near-virgin and abandoned farmland threatened to encroach upon the edges of the city limits. The *monte* that was a few miles out from Araceli's house engorged like a poisoned heart, bounding toward civilization branch by branch.)

Felix would keep this figure a secret from his peers. While other kids spoke of El Cucuy or La Llorona coming to snatch them from their families if they misbehaved, Felix listened like an outsider. These cultural monsters never spooked him like they did some other children. Not like his sometimes-best friend Carlos who, if provoked long enough, would begin to cry out for his mother, prompting the teacher to escort him to the counselor's hand-in-hand. These monsters were always skirting reality. The dark figure outside the *monte* contradicted them with its shadowy presence. He had seen it with his own eyes.

On a stagnant day in school when the clouds hung heavy, pregnant with rain, Ms. Orozco, the young fourth grade teacher of whom most of the faculty thought of as an overcompensated babysitter, decided to ebb the tiny sea of unbound child-talk, now intensified with the promise of rain, by assigning a journal entry. Over the chorus of groans, Ms. Orozco issued the prompt while passing out loose-leaf paper: "What Thanksgiving means to me." For journal entries, Ms. Orozco stipulated that each student must write at least one page's worth of near-perfect prose, employing words her kids had been learning that week; complete sentences were a must; and although on-topic writings were encouraged, she believed in the liberties of scribing another story in lieu of overall topical consistency.

Leaves rattled pockets of static from the stirring wind as Felix stumbled at the tiered steps of each empty line on the paper before him. In one corner of the classroom, high and leering above the door that opened out to the outdoor hallway, perched a rounded mirror through which Felix stole glimpses of his classmates. Jessica sat in front of him, turning her paper over to continue writing at the top of the back. Always a risk-taker, Hector glided his hand from point to point on his paper, undoubtedly drawing recreations of comic strips lining the insides of his dad's *Hustler* while sitting right across Ms. Orozco's desk. Felix gleamed Ms. Orozco for a split second. She must have noticed Hector's manic and frighteningly accurate imitations by now. Her head had bowed forward as if asleep. Upon a second look at the corner mirror, however, Felix discerned the browning leaves of a paperback resting on Ms. Orozco's lap.

At the back of the class, Felix could hear the clenching of teeth, toes, butts and feel the thickening of the classroom atmosphere when Ms. Orozco began writing names on the chalkboard. To earn a participation grade for the week, one had to read aloud from their journal entry. Among the list of names, Felix found himself in the middle, preceding Hector Olivares, now glazed with sweat at the front of the class. A light humidity arose, building itself from his classmates' collective perspiration. Suddenly the empty lines on his paper began to break. Rosa Liscano was called upon to read. One bullet dodged. Why couldn't they outline their hands like they did in earlier grades, creating bedraggled turkeys that served as classroom wallpaper? From his inner cubby of disdain, Felix overheard Ms. Orozco correct Rosa when she lapsed into what Ms. Orozco called "a passive language."

"But Miss, I couldn't think of a word for *pardo*," Rosa pleaded her case.

Felix was thankful for Rosa's unwitting distraction. The sound of rustling leaves reached into his mind with soft fingers.—There must be a story he could tell.—The sound morphed into lapping waves on a beach. She was there, still unformed, still shadowed by unknowing.—His roving tongue began to pick at his teeth.—Did he taste sand?

Ms. Orozco asked Rosa to sit as she began choosing another

name from the board.

Static. Static like shifting sands. Static in the head…

Felix didn't speak in Spanish because his parents talked to him in English; his parents thought that their cultural language would be seen as obsolete and perish; and so, when Felix asked, "Who are you?" without any trace of an accent, Ernesta would smile knowing that her cousin didn't want her son to speak the language that cursed him. It was a weighted smile, but a smile of legacy, as if she was a suspicion that needed heeding.

Taking a chance on her nephew's speech, she told him to call her Tia. But he had heard that word used from his friends, though still vague on its entire meaning.

"That means we're related, right?" he said. "Tia means we're related."

Before she could hold her emotions at dubious length, Ernesta felt warmth and excitement, and immediately wanted to cry; but she caught herself and only said, "Yes," later adding that he could not tell his mother about her because it would make both of them sad. He promised not to.

Unbeknownst to his mother, Felix would continue to meet with his Tia for several weeks, dipping, unnoticed, from his friends, into the *monte* at the end of the road leading north. His Tia always astounded him with her stories of how things were before his mother gave birth to him. She told about travels on unpaved roads and about the people that traveled them; and how only recently they covered some roads with tar so you can know that it leads somewhere someone has been to before. All the while she spoke to him, she would dip into Spanish and repeat herself in English, but Felix wouldn't catch on sometimes, so he thought that she kept secrets from him. It wasn't long before Felix wanted his Tia to teach him some Spanish since his parents and teachers didn't. She agreed to, but on condition that he couldn't speak any in front of his mother. He asked her if it would make her sad again, to which Ernesta nodded. "You must really care for my mom if you never want to make her sad."

Felix's hidden relationship wouldn't remain so past the second month following its commencement. A few of Felix's friends from down the way would witness the boy venture into the *monte*, accompanied by some shadowy stranger. They peeled away to the Maldonado house, catching their breath by the front door. The dust barely began to settle about their feet before Araceli's visage changed from the initial pleasure at seeing her son's friends to a muted volatility. Her eyebrows arched, and the corners of her mouth flattened. Her nostrils flared as she pushed past the children, the *chanclas* clapping at the balls of her heels.

The green-striped housedress whipped in the wind now gathered momentum in a brewing thunderstorm. As Araceli approached the *monte*, she could discern the two figures lounging on a felled tree trunk. Felix turned to his mother as if from a dream. She couldn't possibly be here. This was a domain free from constraints. He couldn't imagine his mother being a part of this world. But she held out her hand, beckoning him to join her. She didn't need to say anything. Felix turned to his Tia who nodded in the direction out of the monte. Felix kept looking back at the presence in the wood.

Felix knew not how his mother found out, and he verbally fought her, cursing her for taking his Tia away from him, when, in essence, she was taking him away from her. And when she heard "Tia," she nearly collapsed on her knees; but the buckling adversely reinforced her forbiddance.

Araceli scarcely let Felix out of her sight from that point forward. Her eyes followed him everywhere. If he stepped outside, she would lean against the facade of the house. He would feel her gaze superimposed on the sky if he were to walk to one of his friend's houses, or when he went to school; or even in the slight cracks between the closed door to his room at night. If he were to look up from his meal at the dinner table, his eyes would meet hers, sometimes a moth flittering into place on the wall behind her, wings expansive and cloth-like, with dark symmetrical circles, gray and brown like mesquite knots.

He would never forget his conversations with his Tia in the *monte*. He would become restless under his mother's watch; his dreams and his heart stirred with a longing for the connection between him and his Tia Ernesta, for the magic she spoke of, and the new thoughts and language she taught him—all of which, he surmised, seemed destructive to his mother. In one foul swipe she severed the ties between him and what he might have called family. From then on, Felix treated Araceli with distance, a distance which seemed to hunger for more distance, until Felix's adolescent presence silenced the space around him if he was to share it with his mother.

Felix became rebellious in high school. He grew an intolerance to his teachers' and classmates' clean and proper language; so not only was he silent at home, the invisible bubble of which stifled his family at the dinner table or on car rides traveled with him into the classroom. Unable to adopt their tongue, Felix quit school completely, subsequently quitting the Maldonado house to work on King's Ranch with Hector Olivares, who had graduated from drawing naked women on college ruled paper to occupying his time thinking of ways to obtain another paper. "Who needs school when we can start making money *now*," seemed like a good enough mantra for two teenagers splitting from home as Uncle Sam sent Nixon packing, August 1974.

| * |

Many years later, when the palpitations of her heart rattled her veins and her body complete, Araceli would have considered forgiving her cousin Ernesta had she not already let the reins of that beaten and furious horse loose over the interim of Felix's growth, her grandson's conception, and her husband's fall in combat during the U.S. invasion of Panama.

Her parents had just passed away: Leocadia in her sleep; Fernando a few months after from heartache: yet she still saw them when she returned to the house of her childhood. She saw them in the small things they left behind—she saw her husband the same way; and she deduced that the world only consists of these things. She thought of her Tio Humberto, still in search somewhere in Mexico. Perhaps now he is a myth. Araceli saw him, too, in the blue map, the nonsensical scribble-work his face, or his heart.

While examining the map in her old room, she noticed a circle of light adjacent on the wall. She put her hand to it, watched how it momentarily bleached her skin, and turned to see its origin. There rested on a slant the mirror of her childhood, the silver in the back considerably deteriorated, revealing portions of the mirror for glass— but it was hers. She held it to her chest.

Out the open window, under a sky of rolling clouds sheathing and unsheathing a delicate sun, she saw Ernesta's old shed and made her way to it.

Inside, she noticed how clean it was, as if someone continued to live there. Had her parents known?

There was a bed with holy, old sheets, and she could see the lumps in the mattress; the dresser that her father built for Ernesta with a jewelry box on top of it; and a small window with white curtains spread apart, admitting inward the soft light of the sun.

Araceli went to the box, inspected it, and found a mirror inside. A mirror and nothing else. She placed it back, went to the open entrance, and looked out into the landscape. Everything seemed illumined. She felt sweat begin to bead and run down her face. She didn't feel hot. Wind blew at the tall weeds at the sides of her parents' house. Then she couldn't seem to feel the smile on her face—though she was smiling—and she couldn't wipe the sweat from her brow.

Nearly a half-hour later, she opened her eyes and beheld Ernesta. Her cousin held her head up by placing it on her lap. Ernesta was running her fingers through Araceli's hair.

Araceli couldn't help but to notice the sparkling tears in her cousin's eyes; she felt them splash on her forehead; felt the wind breeze over them and how cool it felt; felt them dry on her skin but melt into her. She couldn't help but to remember how she suspected Ernesta of calling her a witch, when it was her son, in all his resentment, who did and relayed it to her grandson.

She felt that the curse fled from her, had escaped her some time ago; that if she was to die, she would die alone.

Araceli delicately said, "I am sorry we never had the chance to forgive each other."

Ernesta sniffled and felt her throat tighten. "Don't die," she demanded. "Don't die. Please. You know what's going to happen."

"I can't help it. I feel my heart is bursting."

"Why do you sound so calm about it?"

"Because I forgive you."

"You idiot!"

"You can have everything that belongs to me. The house is yours. It will be empty, but it is yours. I don't know why I realize this now. You had no family to call your own."

"You idiot—I have been living in an empty house all this

time—I don't need yours—you idiot—*don't die!*"

Ernesta's face was a mesh of solitude and sadness.

Araceli: "It's something out of my control. Like my birth. Like yours.

"Please, tell me a story, Ernesta."

Ernesta sniffed the snot back into her nose, her hot eyes searching around her. Her trembling hands ran through her cousin's hair, eventually matting it down with the rich oils of her fingers.

"There once were two princesses—"

"Can one of them be me?"

"Yes, of course! They brushed each other's hair and—"

"Can the other one be you? I want it to be you."

Ernesta felt Araceli's head lose its uprightness. She felt that she only cradled her cousin's head and, therefore, the last thoughts of words and images—then nothingness, then peaceful sleep.

She thought she heard the *monte* yawn from a distance.

Araceli's lips, thin and partly open, had turned blue despite the golden lionhead of the sun now reddening at the western gate of the sky. The two cousins kept this pose.

When Araceli's last breath had exited her lungs, a light shone onto Ernesta's face. It was the mirror, held in Araceli's inanimate hand, reflecting the light of the sun until a roaming cloud sheathed it. For that instant of shrouded clarity, Ernesta saw herself in the mirror, and she saw, beneath her face, her sleeping cousin and how similar they looked.

EL REY:
REY PECINA & THE HAND
OF DISCREATION

Of course she wants to get a job.

I hate that I can't get away from the thought even at work. I already jabbed into a pallet last week with the lift. Super yelled at me, What's the deal, Pecina? Just these thoughts, boss. Nothing. Then he hits me with the, Need me to cut your days? So you can hang out with school kids at your daytime? Like it's my fault I wanna make an extra buck. But I took it, I said, No, sir. No need…

Christ. Don't I do enough for her? Get everything she needs?

She should understand how good she has it. Maybe this house ain't it, sure. The houses she has in mind have yards and trees you plan for and stone fences and they look real tall from the outside; then when you go inside there comes the wife sort of gliding down the stairs like a ghost. But those are neighborhoods without trailers. I promised her I'd get us out. Doesn't that mean enough for her? But no, she gotta go outside and fetch some money for herself.

And Clari wants her to go through with it. Like I give a shit about what my own sister says. I don't know where she gets these big ideas from—the both of them. The tools are laid out before them. There are maps to things that you can't change. They think they can bring California here, or New York. I've seen the videos. I've seen the frames of those crazy lesbians with wild hair asking for more of everything. That's where they get it from, thinking this place can change, when if they just looked at it for a minute, they can see how easy it could be. Instead, you got what'shisface who's dating Clari—I don't know how still—living with the insecurity of her being able to live without him. That's why I have to maintain. No matter what a liberal says on the internet.

Tells me, I wanna get a job. At the mall of all places. Like hell I'd let her go to some place where other guys can check her out. It's always about the looking. I've been a man most of my life—I know what goes on beyond the eyes. We stare holes into things until we're caught. There's no getting around it. Shit, I've caught guys on the job looking at nudes sitting between pallets like it's some private hole.

They can look. As long as they don't look at mine.

I told her when I got back from Mexico that I'd take care of us. I do us so many favors. And it's not like I wanted to go. Like all hell did I want to go fish my nephew out of that hell uncensored on Facebook. I did her the favor of not telling her shit how they walked holding hands in a straight line not knowing where their parents went not knowing not knowing like ten yards out hearing the rust thwack into the neck not knowing all experience of parenthood gone all gods gone just mask and glove of discreation I had to make up a lie. I had to lie about not seeing the black trash bag twisted up like a candy wrapper for something the size of my own… about not seeing the envelope in the washing machine, and about not giving it to Hector while I went with him to Mexico City. About not wanting to take him with me. About not wanting to stay there with the rest of my dad's family for him. Those lies are another dude's life. Not mine. We met one day four years ago. Since then, I can't say that was me. Everyone has to stay the way I see them or don't. I don't know how to make them. I thought it'd be money. And now this.

fuck fuck fuck

Pecina—go wash your face or something before I really kick your ass outta here.

Shithead thinks he can boss me around like that like he runs the place. I'll take it, but only because I'm too distracted. Maybe looking at the shitty bathroom will get my mind off it. Christ, it's like they never clean in here. The light's crusted over—with what I don't know. The urinal's always about to overflow. The toilet seat's always about to slide off and take you off with it. And the mirror, Christ, the mirror can't give anything besides some salty language and a version of yourself all stained in water. I dream of pristine toilets…

I can't believe she told me that. The nerve. I told her, You think I'm stupid or something I said I don't want no scaly motherfuckers giving you an eye They only have one thing on their mind I said One thing.

I know how she'll listen. It always works somehow. I don't mean to do it but I suddenly feel her wrist in my grasp and I'll look her straight in the eye and there outside of everything she's been told about being a new woman she'll understand me and feel the grip of a man that works for his I can barely see my eyes through all this graffitti

And I'll leave it like that. I'll keep her wrist locked in my hand *where it belongs*

She has her place Mama has her place

She caught my wrist before another clumped up fist hot and sweaty landed on her Clari was in the backseat not saying anything There was rain but the sun was so bright I could see her and me so clear like ghosts on the windshield that was clouding over with our breath

Our breath was hot in the car How she didn't retaliate was beyond me

Clari was busy not saying You can't do anything to him Her

knowing what was in me That even at the age of nine there rose in me a wrath but I

He told me boys are different anyways

He won't listen to you she didn't say

She looked like him holding her by the wrist to drag her from place to place Now it was getting hard to feel my hand And Clari in the back busy not saying anything Is my hand disappearing

Did she grip my hand with the glove of discreation

My wrist slipped from her fingers onto her lap and she began to cry

She has her place Even if she has to hide away from me when she cries I have no tolerance for that She can cry all she wants but it wont make me stop

I hate her I remember hating her for making him leave

I used to like it when he took me out just the two of us I liked watching him shave in the mirror before taking me to school You could tell there was a pride in things he did as a man

One day he hit her square in the face for no reason me and Clari saw

The black trash bag rustled

He lost his job and kept on swearing Fuck this Fuck that Dont look at me Dont like there was something in our eyes he couldnt bear

Clari started crying

Mama looked to the floor not looking at anything Her face looked like it was melting like someone put a fire underneath her face

Clari started *crying*

But where were the tears Looking into this shitty bathroom mirror and I realize I've never cried for her or for him for that matter. Not a thing to cry about, maybe. Never saw him shed one tear even in the moments when it made sense. You lose a whole house while some day traders somewhere get the deal of a lifetime, or many lifetimes. I can see you crying over that, but not you, Dad. Not even when your own mother died from an aneurysm that made like a second brain taking over did you cry for her. Not even on the last day you said goodbye to me and Clari and ditched back to Mexico to live with some cousins and their crackhead driving knowing full well what you were walking into when you went. But you went *and the black trash bag rustled all of them lined up orphaned by a machete rusted over by rain and weeds and now blood the bodies*

and I promised never to hit Mom anymore even if to myself even if I never visit her even as Clari brings it up every time I see her *like I give a damn about what my sister says* and I saw Flor in the mirror looking at herself her face the spitting image of her own mother who says I'm no good Flor's face under that light her cheek shiny from crying fuck fuck fuck

I told her everything is going to be okay. That everything will be taken care of, as long as you give me a chance. And she goes on about the burden of living in a patriarchal state. More liberal propaganda. Goes on about how it hurts me, that I do too much that it's crushing me. Why can't we keep things the same? *i see them line up for the bus the late afternoon like a crushed grapefruit all of them under it after school waiting for the bus eyeing my uniform me making sure they stay on the curb yanking them by their backpacks if they try me and step onto pavement i dont like it i dont like it i have to keep them from*

Pecina, the hell is keeping ya? Do I need to dock your pay for you to get out of that damn toilet?

He leans forward, puts his hand on my shoulder. Gets real close so that I can smell his potato chip breath.

I could get any of these Mexicans to take your place and they'll work like machines at half your pay. Now get out.

My face feels hot. . .

But how do you keep your household in line? I asked him. He pretended to be busy on his tablet like he always is.

Managing that is like managing you guys here. You gotta be stern, an authority. Otherwise, what's the point in being a man? Don't look out into the world for change. Get your household in order. It's good housekeeping.

He looked up from his glowing tablet. First time we've made eye contact since I got hired.

It looks like you're really struggling with this. Listen, it benefits me to have you straight when you work. These fruits won't treat themselves. Unless you keep losing them like you have, that is. If the house needs affirmation and you fail to fulfill your duties as a man, then you're no good to me here. Now, I hope you take that and come back tomorrow straight. Finish the shift. And goddamn do we have to change y'all's restroom. Mine up in the office looks like a magazine compared to this shithole.

I followed him out. He was keeping ahead of me in the pockets where the light panels didn't shine and I could see his tablet bobbing away then up the stairs where it hid behind blinds.

"ALWAYS TIME ENOUGH": JOSUE NIEBLEZ NEVER THOUGHT TO GET A LIBRARY CARD

He awoke from a dream. He has had it before. It's of him, now in his fifties, and of his grandmother, who outlived her spouse and her six sons. It's unknown to him whether she still lives or not, though time would count her with one hundred and thirty years if she does; and if he did find that she does, it wouldn't surprise him.

The dream always finds him sitting before her, as he grew accustomed to, even in his subconscious, in the middle of a game she played with him when he was a boy, before his father passed away from a cottonmouth bite.

A marble the color of his grandmother's glassy eyes overtaken by cataracts stood inert on a coffee table that seemed to belong to her old house located on the family ranch outside Tiempo, though he wouldn't guess as to whose house they occupied during the dream. It seemed familiar, yet dream-generated, as the interior took the shape of his grandmother's living room, but it seemed shipwrecked with the sun breaking through the window, drowning them in an intestinal color. Pruned and sunken-eyed, his grandmother commanded most of his attention with her timeworn body, the faint scent of aloe vera reminiscent to him of the long summer days in his childhood.

The marble tempted him the way it tempted him forty years ago, but as soon as he unfolded his arm to reach for it, she sheltered the object from him with a wooden cup. She would laugh and say to him in a toothless Spanish, "You spend so much time trying to obtain this marble that you are losing your dreams." It almost sounded to him like an imprecation.

The dream would end when his grandmother retrieved the marble back to the pocket of her bonnet-print nightgown, her attention fixed on him, almost as if she could see through the haze of her eyes.

He has had the dream before, so Josue Nieblez wasn't surprised to awake from it, though what startled him surrounded him: The Tiempo Library, originally built for the reason that a shipment of books no official recalled ordering, arrived one day in the city's distant past. He forgot how he arrived there, and he considered the possibility of his dream projecting him across the temporal-geographical plane; but slowly his memory revisited him like echoes of consciousness; and the memories spoke *arrived at the library took a while like it usually does to get out of the car still dont have help dont need help wish everyone looked at me different cant open door regular push the button saw them walk past me pushing myself feel like a drifting island* and then he figured he must have fallen asleep, cutting the recollection short.

The agitation of waking up from a public nap washed on his face. Fluorescent lights racked his vision until it settled on the hushed commons where ribbons of arpeggiated keystrokes swam through the shelves, accentuated by the sound of footfalls cascading from patrons ambling leisurely through intimate halls. It was the latter—this noise that became dizzying.

'If God thought of everyone equal, he would've made everyone with no legs. Or at least keep it the same and then take them away from us all, that way we can all realize what we had and what we wouldn't anymore.'

Josue Nieblez's brown, lackluster eyes watched legs pass by him in the muted bustle of the library. Rising more and more, the now cacophony of footsteps banked and ebbed on his chest, to which his breathing, his very existence fought perhaps not out of defiance, but more closely out of annoyance.

'If only that goddamn accident didn't happen in the middle of my life—if only it had happened earlier, then maybe. . .

'I can't blame anyone for this. At times, when I'm really reaching, I can't even come to point the finger at the son-of-a-bitch that clipped me. To think that it's already been a year since it happened—and it still hurts. But it's not the kind of pain like headaches. It's something different entirely. And I know what it is.

'If anyone, I'll blame God. He runs the show, doesn't he? At what point did he decide that I deserve to lose more? It's so funny that I can't even laugh.'

Josue Nieblez noticed his chest rising and falling, the fibers of his navy-blue shirt stretching with each inhale. When he looked to his chest, it was inevitable for him to peek at his inanimate legs; and he considered in cheeky self-derision whether putting pants on was necessary anymore. With this little thought, he became calmly and mildly angry. No one would be able to tell from his already hardened face, but behind that stiff flesh brewed a storm.

'Come on. Move, goddammit. What's the good in keeping you around? I might as well be carrying around lead. You're real fucking heavy you know that? Why did I ever agree to keep you? *Move*, dammit!'

He lifted a fist into the air as if to strike his knee, but he realized where he was and what he would be doing. Looking up, he saw a young couple staring at him, a boy and a girl. The boy with lips oddly pursed said to him in Spanish, "Are you trying to make it work?" and let out a chortle. The girl fought back a laugh, hit her companion on the arm, and reprimanded him.

Josue Nieblez glared at them both and said to no one through tight teeth, "Damn kids."

| * |

He was moving through the maze of shelves, the smell of the books potent and omnipresent. His eyes rolled past titles and authors; and while spines scrolled over the arcs of his eyes, the mind, too, sought for some memory buried in itself.

I assure you that I know what I'm talking about, he recalled Marci telling him. If those degrees up there aren't indications enough, I have written books on the subject. Feel free to check one out on your own time. Our time today is done.

He had gotten so used to addressing her by her first name that he forgot her last name. It wasn't that he didn't trust her credibility. No one he knew actively went to therapy. The problems of the mind lay like specters in the backdrop of consciousness, never to surface in conversation. What did it mean to draw out the mind and inspect it? Inspection was no mystery to him: His years in the service always functioned under scrutiny; and before that, his own father ran the house like a drill sergeant. Even as a vet, during the time he headed his own lawn care business, inspection meant intense detail. For example, a certain percentage of dead leaves blown off the driveway, every shrub rounded, no loose weed reached for the mailbox. Inspection meant looking out for abnormalities. What was wrong with his mind?

My thinking is square, doc, he told her once. It's these damn legs that's the problem.

The more eye contact he made with her, the more he felt something else was there. Not that she didn't believe him.

What I'm suggesting, she said, is that a lot of people need some sort of *object*…

His hands resigned on his wheels. The decades-formed callouses flushed softly on the rubber.

Lost between two aisles, his eyes lifted from one shelf to the other. He suddenly confronted the section dedicated to the Rio Grande Valley's writers. There, on one of the top shelves, he gleaned a book whose title curved at the top-center, rounding a drawing of a full moon low above an old chapel. While the words were unintelligible to him from his vantage point, he knew the artwork—knew before memory caught up. He gripped the rubber once more and moved closer to the book with unbreakable attention.

Once at the foot of the shelf, Josue Nieblez glanced at his surroundings and, secure in his momentary privacy, pushed himself up with one arm and reached for a book with the other. 'If only I could knock it down at least,' he thought as he strained his side, only able to flick the yawning paperback cover before he fell back to his seat red-faced.

The miniature moon hung high as he buried his forehead into his palm and remained that way for a spell. Josue Nieblez found himself returning to the table at which he napped earlier, oblivious to the looks other people gave him.

'I'd hate to ask her for another. It's so shameful. But after the accident, I just started throwing things away—almost everything. Everything except the memories of her and her mother. Goddammit. I can't believe I lost them both.'—his eyes began to seek for an empty space to escape to in his mind—'And no matter how hard I try to cover it up, them being gone from me still comes and hurts me. They're both gone. *Mi vieja y mi luz*. Gone…' His eyes found empty space in a hollow corner. His brow like a brush of bereavement sank with gravity, giving an air to him of fury and melancholy.

| * |

It was late in the morning when the young reporter, Tyler Lucio, would enter the Tiempo Library, breeze by the aisles, neglecting Faulkner and Hemingway, tiptoe to obtain a book, and pass by a silvery steel table with a man sitting in a silvery steel chair at the head. He didn't notice it, but the man sitting in the steel chair would wake from some sort of trance, recognize the cover to the book the youth carried, and decide to do something that, by the narrowing of his face, compromised something within.

From behind him, Tyler heard, "Hey, um, kid! Hold on for a second!" He turned around to meet the eyes of the man who gained his attention.

"That book you got there," the man continued, "can I—can I see it?"

Somewhat of a jittery boy, Tyler produced the book with lightly fumbling hands, looked at it, and handed it over to the man.

"Sure."

The man received it with great appreciation, not entirely for the boy but for the circumstances that brought the book to his hands. He examined it half-intensely, half-lovingly, in his hands, finally, the wondrous object that built a bridge to something of importance to him. It had evaded him before like memories tend to do when they are not fresh or practiced; or how objects seem inaccessible, and yet there's the dream of possessing it for as long as one can—and there it was, a link of immaterial possession. Yes, he held the object in his hands; but the intangibility of it lit a pale fire in his chest.

The cover read, "Always Time Enough," the authoress a Bianca Nieblez; and when the man flipped to the dedication, he read a thousand times in one, 'To my Dad who damns everything and loves everyone whether or not he cares to admit it.'

'My Bianca…

'No—not *mine*.

'I wonder if it's lonely up there in the Big Apple. They say you feel the loneliness worse in a big city than in a small one. Ever since she went away on this book—once to teach, the next to live— I've always wondered about that.

'Not mine. I gave her a part of me, and we picked out a name for her, but I can only claim the blood, and she's doing more with it than I have—more than I could ever dream of doing. She is her own person now, and I have no ownership. I've helped raise her, but she chose to be the person she is today. And I'm proud of the person she is today.'

"Um, sir?—are you okay?"

Josue Nieblez returned to the library after wandering off.

"Um, listen, boy: I have to borrow this book. There's no questioning it. You see, this is my daughter's—well, not *this* copy, but she wrote the book. I don't have a copy of my own 'cause I lost it a while ago."

Tyler followed every word and formed an answer: "Take all the time you want. I can always find it somewhere else."

Josue Nieblez nodded, started to think, 'Thank,' and then said, "Thank you."

He began to wheel himself away but quickly and hesitantly rolled back to Tyler, saying, "Can I also borrow your library card?" He checked the pocket of his jeans to retrieve his wallet. "I could pay you." He felt something unfamiliar to him, pulled it out, and examined the marble of his dreams. In the light, it looked clear like a drop of dew, contrary to its perceived color, the color of cloudiness or shroud. He felt that in his pocket he carried his grandmother, and in his hand, his daughter; but he could differentiate between physical possession and that of memory. He began to laugh.

Tyler would refuse the offer.

He lent his card to the man after the man promised to return the book on time. After all, he wouldn't want to be responsible for the book being late.

MALL CHAT:
IF THERE'S ONE THING WILLIAM
LISCANO KNOWS

This way and that; downward and awayward; roving at the doomscroll; tailing tail; discerning the peripheral body until only limbs appeared to swim across color and floaters sliding across it all—sometimes longtime friends cannot perceive each other sitting around a square table.

"You guys hear about this chick coming down here in the Spring? You wanna hear why she's coming? I'll tell you anyways.

She's coming—all the way from L.A.—to have a picnic in some park somewheres—here in Tiempo of all places—*topless*. I'mma repeat that last part: She's coming down, inviting anybody and everybody to sit in the plain wide open *topless*. Can you believe that? This chick who's got a fucking *body*—I mean, that's what she gets paid for: She wants to do this sort of thing. God bless her."

"Christ, bro. 'That's what she gets paid for?' You can't be saying those things."

"Nambre, it is what it is. She puts out content for guys like me and you and… well *us*. She gets paid, what's the problem?"

"Well, when you put it that way… Wait, no, what do you think about this?"

"Eh, he's not gonna have an opinion on that. Not really part of the code for him, is it?"

"I mean, maybe, you're right. But it still doesn't hurt to ask. Maybe he knows more than us about this."

"She's *obviously* doing this shit for the whole movement, which is commendable. A lot more movements should take these risks. But if she does a thing like this, in the middle of nowhere, especially somewhere where the minds of the people are all… well, like *some* people whose idea of equality is so 20th century, you get monkey balls over here going for the wrong reasons. It defeats the whole fucking purpose. You can't get rid of these things overnight. Also, let's not be fooled by our friend's view of the transaction of beauty."

"Transaction of wuh?"

"Transaction of beauty. You're right insofar as the stipulation is upheld: Someone shows you a beautiful person, that person gets paid by your consumption of the image. That's just business. But if we go past the image, the symbol, what is there? You get the kind of answer that reaches out for equality and better representation and suddenly, the men who were backing you up prefer if you're just a symbol with no meaning behind it. Then you're just a copy of someone who hasn't been realized yet..."

That last voice belongs to a William Liscano, a short, thin, not-too-muscular boy of twenty with calm, tan hands bridged on the small square table in front of him at present. Hardly a reserved fellow, William would rather dictate anything on his mind, answer any question as if practiced, delivering his speech with a detached demeanor. And he made no exception to this conversation located at the food court in the Sunset Mall where everyone else spoke of framed philosophies, albeit not as perfunctory as our boy William. Don't get his delivery wrong, though: He does think a lot, or at least that's what he deduced after having suffered several migraines, the result and ultimate burden of immediate and long-winded opinions that he relates to his three friends: Diego Almaraz (a.k.a. "monkey balls"), David Arguelles, and Tyler Lucio, the latter comrade currently missing from the table.

"Whoa, now. I *know* Goku here sounds like some horndog, but I'm sure he has some other reason he brought this up. And it's not like he's going to that park or anything," David said, coming to aid the friend he's known the longest, or at least provide an opportunity for him. Never one to stomach conflict, especially amongst friends, David Arguelles, like a pensive stone, sits on conversations as a mediator. He could already sense William's austerity toward the subject—much like a handful of other subjects—to which the other sat oblivious, like a child admonished for something it couldn't comprehend.

"Well, maybe I would *like* to go," said the third person in Spanish, eliciting a sigh from David. David's big bearded face concealed his eyes fairly well. They never made contact with others, afraid to offend. Diego's clean-shaven, used-car-salesman face seemed vacant of thought, but open to it. "Look at this guy," he added, "It is like he *does not* appreciate a good pair."

"I'm trying to back you up, Diego," David replied, also in Spanish. "Do you always have to think of these things? I would like to give you more credit one day. It is not always about naked women."

"Well, it looks like I have to compensate for *somebody*," Diego said in English.

William sat back in his chair. "Do you guys always have to go into those *modes*?"

"*Modes*?" Diego said. "It's not *our* fault that you haven't learned what our culture speaks."

William waved his hand in disfavor, like an old man disapproving of soup at a deli, saying, "Get out of here with this culture crap. Just because I'm living in *El Valley* doesn't mean I'm expected to know Spanish, not anymore at least. It's not our culture to know—it's our culture to remember. We're stuck, haven't you heard? Where's Tyler? I'm sure he'll agree with me."

"What to you is the difference between knowing and remembering—" David asked.

Now nauseated with throngs of late Christmas shoppers and associates marching in many directions in chaotic meter, the Sunset Mall hosted the likes of every person. The adults hunted for every deceiving bargain. The children ran around each other, pulling the ends of their parents' clothing asking for the brand-new toy. The boys eyed the girls, the girls the boys, the boys the boys, and the girls the girls. A murmur went about the crowds if heard from a distance, for no one could really hear anyone else without being within close proximity from them. Everything was a mess of flesh and clothing; tan hands, red sweaters, brown faces, blue jeans; blanching legs due to days with no sun; twinkling golden jewelry; sharp and loose blouses and shirts, red, green, white, brown and its variants; *Navidad*.

Amongst the unbroken clamor of shoes, child-yell, and the collective murmur, Diego could hear his friend's distinct voice, a somewhat nasally pretentious tone with hardly any inflection. From his seat, he identified Tyler Lucio from the wall of human, a perpetuating mosaic rippling with the tinsel of gold, silver watches. Tyler was not alone, however. A girl of equal height, striking physiognomy, and short curly brown hair accompanied him.

"Speak of the devil," Diego said as if coming out of a trance.

The other two at the table turned to see Tyler and the girl hug each other, the latter disappearing into the crowds.

As he went to meet with his friends, who stare past him, Tyler at once wonders what they could be looking at, knows, and pulls up a chair, quietly preparing for the interrogation.

"What's *that*?" Diego blurted. The others turned to Tyler with narrowed faces. They wanted to know, too.

Tyler: "A girl."

Diego: "Look, *pendejo*…"

Tyler: "You remember that dating site, um, Please Date Me? Yeah, well, they mailed my girl already—before Christmas."

William, not having it: "What is this, new material? Spill it, newspaper boy."

Tyler: "A'ight, a'ight. I'm pretty sure I've told you guys about Flor." Silence. "Well, either you guys don't listen or you can't read my mind. We've been meeting here since the end of summer." The last word ended like a question.

Diego: "Wait, wait—you mean to tell us that you've had a main squeeze without telling us? Why the silence? I thought we were homies…"

Tyler looked around. "Well, I'm *trying* to keep it under wraps because she's *technically* not mine." The others each expressed something at the same time, sounding like a sighaygueygasp. Tyler took a second look around. "She belongs to the Mary Cone. The

Grand Pan"—he dropped these aliases as if introducing some rap artist—"El Rey." Sighaygueygasp. "It is true."

The source of the "sigh," William began drifting from his friends and out into the crowd. Amidst the blur of passersby stumbled a conspicuously dressed man from a store. The man must have stumbled over his step as he was occupied with his wrist. The vision lifts slightly to reveal Beto's Watch & Repair behind the man, whose outfit piqued interest: the brown slacks, the fitted plaid shirt, the gray sport coat with the elbow patches that tightened as the man fiddled with his watch that had no Bluetooth connectivity, you could tell. While the others talked, William happened to hear Diego saying, "That guy's gonna kill you, bro." 'gonna kill you, bro gonna kill you kill you' William's hands assumed form, bridging together before him, only William began sinking into them, his teeth shut against his knuckles.

"I'm gonna take a piss."

The other three turned to him with squinty eyes like incredulous cats, one of their mouths operating after a trice, Diego: "What, are you waiting for *permission*?"

| * |

The restrooms at the Sunset Mall are always pristine, nearly virginal, as if there is a particular god for public restrooms, and it particularly touches these frequently, for cleanliness is closest to godliness. (It was either this or no one used the facilities at all.) And so, the restroom in which William Liscano entered received the young man like royalty.

Cleanliness notwithstanding, William Liscano couldn't quite relieve himself. He merely stood there not looking at anything, the pristine sheen to everything coating his vision ray after ray until there was a suffocating quality in its brilliance. There was so much to be seen under this white light and white tiles and pearl urinal that any deviating color was conspicuous. He stood like a prop, to be activated by someone else; he needed someone to hit a button so that way he could continue to act normal, to continue to perform like normal.

From the crowds outside the restroom exited a small, sweaty man whose bald head gleamed in the heavenly light the interior of the bathroom emits. The man, heavily mustached, came in singing, the fur atop his upper lip bouncing rhythmically. "FELIZ NAVIDAD. FELIZ NAVIDAD. FELIZ NAVIDAD. PROSPERO ANO Y FELIZIDAD." He did his business at the urinal adjacent to William in the middle of the constant chorus and left without washing his hands, singing, "I WANNA WEESH YOU A MERRY CHREESTMAS." William took it. He didn't question why the man came in to serenade him and his dick. The performance had, however, soothed him enough to finally relieve himself.

William turned the faucet to the sink on and listened as water poured onto the gate of the drain. He pooled some of the water and splashed it onto his face. Looking into the mirror, he noticed a person staring back at him, the only person of his exact appearance, a person William hardly visited only when he decided to look. He stared at the face with intent, measured the likeness to what he imagines himself to look like. This double was an infiltrator whose attention he seemingly could not gain. William knew exactly what the other thought, which made the double's aversion painful.

But once they met eyes, William could see through the temporal tunnel of seasons and years, past measurements of time until the mind settled on a place that transcends history for William: He could see *a city My city Far away from home You'll be scared and lonely and you will miss Tiempo but it never came All those feelings never came until*

In my city existed things not at home Not the fear of having to speak Spanish and being made fun of knowing it but not knowing it Not the humidity that fits on your face like a mask sticky and uncomfortable but you cant take it off no matter how long you remain inside you cant take it off cant escape But I did I escaped and I traded it for my city and my university where they paid me to go and took classes and the people were pleasant as long as you dont get to know them but I did want to get to know him at the party and after his presentation I went up to talk to him and he said that I should meet him at a party and then

fear abashed drowning in something I had never thought about never felt something so exhilarating but he standing in front of a class well-dressed neat hair lips jaw sharp nose eyes lost I am lost in the campus lost in the classroom lost Went to the party talking to him felt found and I knew I knew what I felt knew what I was knew what I had been knew what I am He touched my hand and I couldnt help

i kissed him and at that moment he was mine too like my city like my university all mine

But he backed away and told me words that went against what i did against my feelings against me and suddenly he was never mine but my mind was his It was his and my studies were not but remained mine but i couldnt not after and what he said and soon the university wasnt mine the city wasnt mine

lost travelling home travelling travelling back home—back to Tiempo—back to his mother and father whom did not understand a thing, partly because William never told them how love turns into obsession, less his epiphany of his sexual orientation. The latter amazed him—amazes him still in front of the mirror at the social hub of Tiempo: how it evaded him through childhood and remained reclusive in high school; and then suddenly, it made sense. He arrived at that comprehension when he came back home; and "it made sense" to his friends, at least those of whom he intimated it to, that confession of which felt like a confession but was far from one, since the propensities of a person—some superficial and others covert—are truth and its deviations, incomprehensible to human constructs, but known within the temple of the human soul.

At a blink, William's surroundings travelled back to him from the recesses of the present. He felt his face drip and ran his hand across it. His phone vibrated in his pocket.

"grab me a coffee fool"

He rolled his eyes.

| * |

It was a new coffee shop in a wave of new coffee shops in the Rio Grande Valley, only this one had the luxury of renting a stall at the Sunset Mall. A rank of various flags suspended by wire overhead—flags of Texas and Mexico, one regular American flag, another in black and white with a blue streak running across the cloth, a yellow flag depicting a coiled snake—all of these hid a steel factory wall with frames of men in uniform. Before these portraits of eagle visages, a sales clerk with equally striking physiognomy stood amidst coffee paraphernalia and a cash register. Most of the seating was located in the storefront, as a line formed that stretched in ugly discordance from the register to the front door of local coffee enthusiasts wielding phones and snapping pictures which, once posted to a social media platform, will receive the caption, "something new ig lol."

The sight was met with William's immediate aversion. He produced his phone from his pocket in an attempt to escape the spectacle with memes ostensibly mocking the ideologies behind the flags hanging above him like slates of sugar glass. Some customers lingered in the shop after placing their order, inspecting yellow mugs and T-shirts branding a snake coiled around a cup of what can only be presumed to be coffee.

With only a few more patrons ahead of him, William

discerned voices rising from the cash register. He joined others in the shop lingering around the merchandise in subtly turning their eyes toward what sounded like conflict.

"Listen, sir," said a customer, at a noticeably calm volume, as if aware of an accumulating crowd. "All I want is an iced coffee."

"I know what you *want*," rebutted the barista, heavily bearded and folding his arms across his chest, flexing his muscles in one sustained contraction. "What you *want* is to change the way we do business around here. I'll tell you something, though: Our shop here is a response to your agenda."

"My agenda? You're getting riled up over a sticker on my phone, man."

"Don't call me that like you're comfortable with me."

The customer at the head of the line took an audible pause, that pause in which one checks their periphery to make sure they are still existing in reality and not some internet post. William felt the pause with a crushing guilt and likewise gauged the room. Everyone else in the shop grew quiet—increasingly so after the initial point of conflict—and averted their attention to their little, stupid activities. William dropped his gaze to his phone once again, scrolling and finding nothing, nothing, nothing—

"Well, the way I see things—"

William didn't realize those words came from him. The young man in queue with him turned around and searched his eyes, while the barista sized him up like a prize fighter.

But why stop here

"You're missing out on a customer and, might I add, a growing demographic. It doesn't make sense for you—I'm assuming you own this business, and the men behind you are your daddies: It doesn't make sense to close yourself off from that market. You're getting hung-up on these symbols when at the end of the day you have to go home and put food on the table. Doing stuff like this kinda impedes on that just a bit, don'tcha think?"

The barista flexed his pecs. "These brave men are not my 'daddies'"—air quotes—"They fought for my country. Something you have no idea about."

"My mom did two tours in Afghanistan," the other said in a monotone. "She reminds me every day about her service." There's a far-away-ness to his tilted vision.

"My point is," William continued, "just take his money. It doesn't behoove you to be a jerk like this."

From a side door behind the bar emerged this stalky character, Santa Clause-like in stature, from the beard and belly to the reading glasses resting on the nostrils. "We got a problem out here, son?" Santa asked, the words finding light from the forest of mustache hair.

The "son" eyed the two infiltrators, then the rest of the crowd who at present silently replaced the shop's merchandise where they found it.

"No, no problem." He flashed a smile to Santa. "That'll be eight dollars, man."

"For a *small*?"

A shrug. "That's inflation for you."

Santa sniffed to clear a nostril and, before returning to his five-by-five office to crunch the numbers and scroll through the memes, said into the air, "Happy holidays, everybody."

There's a more than audible sigh from the queue.

| * |

The conversation had shifted when William returned to his friends, though the focus remained on Tyler who sat back in his chair, arms folded, eyes set at the center of the table. There was something *there*, at the center of the table, that Tyler could see that his friends could not. William has read this look on other's faces before.

"But tell me, bruh: What would you be gaining if you left the newspaper? You, yourself, have told us time and time again that somebody needs to tell these stories."

William didn't expect such poignancy from Diego. It seemed to pierce into Tyler as it might have surprised him, too.

"Yeah, well, you're not surrounded by this shit, are you?" Tyler responded, his eyes, his entire burden of reason and empathy, now tracking Diego's. "It's day-in-day-out with these stories that no one seems to care about." Diego waved his hand at it. "No, it's true. You think the rest of the country cares about us? How about the rest of Texas? Fuck, I doubt *you* read my shit." Diego turned away, breaking their eye contact. "And this shit follows you, man. I can hardly think about anything else. I feel helpless. For a culture that doesn't treat me like I exist. And that's one thing. But there's also groups of people who either can't be themselves, or can't even be in this country, for Chrissake. You tell me why this matters."

After a short silence, David asked, "Is that why you sometimes tell us about leaving?"

Sitting across from Tyler, William recognized something in the heaviness of his friend's brow. When the spirit sinks, the body follows suit. His hands were knotted underneath his arms, and they rose with his chest full of shallow breaths. The shoulders climbed upwards until the neck nearly vanished beneath the shadow of the chin. The rubber of his shoes tapped incessantly on the concrete, granting the audience a glimpse into what must have been going on behind the face. The lips were busy as the teeth worked the gums raw. The eyes cast an empty vision somewhere, anywhere away. The overcast eyebrows failed to hide this faraway look.

Reclaiming his seat, oblivious to a crooked look Diego gave him, William inhaled deeply and began: "You look nauseous, comrade. Are these assholes ribbing ya?" He took an airy drink from a straw.

"Where's my coffee, asshole?" Diego asked, sitting up from his chair.

"It wasn't even that good, don't worry about it." William said this without making eye contact with the friend he surely injured.

"It's the same thing we talk about every other day, Willie. Nothing too concerning," Tyler said. He drew the skin of his thumb to his teeth, giving his gum some respite. The body is quick to discard the flesh for dead when stress courses through the mind like an infiltrator.

"You usually keep quiet when we talk about this." Diego's arms were now folded as his eyes remained immoveable from William, who, to this second, hadn't so much as peaked at Diego. "Go ahead and give him your list of reasons why Tiempo sucks and why he should leave." This was turning into something more than an empty cup of iced coffee. Typically, at the defense of his friends, David resolved to remain quiet during the exchange, the point of his beard a hairy compass settled on William. The endearingly innocent face became critical.

"Sometimes, Ty, it'll seem like no one's on your side," William started, not looking anywhere, or at anyone. "I've felt that way; and I've felt that way for a very long time. And you'll feel like going away will make things better; that suddenly, you'll find yourself out there in some unfamiliar place. I'll tell you one thing that was true to me: I only disappeared further when I got out there; and I found what justice meant out there for people like me; and I found that it ain't much different. You're always pushing against something that's doing its best to squish you into obedience. But, simultaneously, I'm glad I left. I got the chance to receive this insight, or what I think might be an insight. Another thing I know: When I came back knowing what I know about myself, there were only a few people I could trust carrying that information. Remember when I was telling you? Fuck, we were at that protest against LNG. Fucking hot that day. Remember?" There was a boylike curl to his lip as nostalgia intercepted his speech.

"Yeah, Willie. You were freaking out because you thought your parents were gonna kick you out."

The two laughed at this memory.

"And I remember what you said to me. You said that even if they did, you'd let me live at your place. I was shocked, not that you were such a good friend, but also that you offered your sofa for me to sleep in."

"Ah hell, man," Diego interjected. "That sofa's older than my grandma, and it smells worse, too!"

"Hey, wait a minute," Tyler began defending himself, "I remember offering you my bed, you jackass."

"Oh, that's right!" William said, his index finger raised to the ceiling. "You said we could share the same bed. Just no gay shit. Verbatim."

"Well, no one's perfect," Tyler responded with a wily smile.

WATCHMAN / WATCH OUT MAN: ROLANDO FLORES TELLS A STORY, EVERYONE LISTENS

"He inhales to laugh."

The words read aloud into the empty office of the Tiempo Eagle sound like a threat; they vaulted over every cubicle with waning success, dipping into the pockets of communal workspaces occupied by his colleagues but a few hours ago. All had retired from the hive and into their sunset privacy, exiting one-by-one the stone building erected initially as a panaderia/tax office combination in the sixties. At the time, the Tiempo Eagle shared space with a credit union near the downtown area, up the street from the Tequila Worm. The move northward developed when a fire engorged itself of all the pan dulce and, eventually, as fires are apt to do, the whole panaderia/tax office combo. (In an interview featured in the paper the next day, the owner of the panaderia, pictured with knuckles folded over a baseball cap in front of the blackened establishment, couldn't imagine the source of the fire; but if he were to take a guess, the prime suspect would have to have been the *marranitos*.) This coincided with the buying-out of the credit union and, eventually, as Big Business is apt to do, the space for Tiempo's local paper by a then-burgeoning national bank. Contractors remodeled and rebuilt over what foundation remained of the charred panaderia/tax office. And to this day, if chanced upon, one may take a whiff of pan dulce lingering in the air, commingling with the smell of fresh print.

Tyler drew breath and could discern the scent of *conchas* basking in some invisible corner of the dark office. Behind and high above him loomed an arrangement of clocks displaying times from various parts of the world. At present, a Japanese reporter must be stepping out for lunch.

The white glow of his monitor shone as a beacon in the now darkened office. An empty text space taunted Tyler. He has yet to transfer his words from the notes he jotted onto his legal pad, as well as an audio recording taken on his phone. Pressing play on the audio file instantly brought him to the meeting he had with Rolando Flores yesterday, and how, at his first impression of the man in the flesh,

Rolando howled with laughter, the kind of laughter that elicits unease in the room. "You don't expect that from a guy like him," he remembered Quintanilla saying to him once, prior to the interview.

"Q. told me he looked like a *Chino*," Tyler began to read from his notes, "'like someone he saw in a Jackie Chan movie.' I guess R. F. has to have some sense of humility when interacting with civilians. Ex-military. You can see the oblong dog tags pressing through the Hawaiian shirt. He says he loves Hawaiian shirts. Apparently, they hold some nostalgic value from service. Twenty-eight and unmarried. Homebody. Difficulty keeping eye contact. Will periodically glance outside the bar window to his Kia parked at the meter. The Kia piques interest. I asked him about the bumper stickers."

The reading and the audio matched each other. It seemed to him like a play, as if beyond the actuality of it, there formed a theatricality in the reception. He imagined heavy, red curtains parting, opening up to the memory.

Rollie: "Oh, you mean the anime characters? That was a holdover from my time in Japan. Pretty cool nation, that Japan. A whole sea of the same people living on this island. Good Christians, too. Did you know that? It isn't all Buddhism or any of that mumbo jumbo. They've been pretty busy since we, y'know, dropped the bombs on them. I actually watched a lot of anime over there—and a lot ever since." (*He has small eyes. I can see why Q. ribbed him on that.*) "I'm sure we can talk about anime all day. You must have grown up on the stuff—"

Tyler: "I know some of those characters. I was just surprised you had *those*—" (*I was referring to the female characters with impossible breasts. Juxtapose that with the typical male protagonists—*)

Tyler skimmed past this section, flipped the yellow page.

Rollie: "Most people who know me, who know the work I do, are kind of put-off by that. They can't *square* it. Nowadays, people will throw the baby with the bathwater, as they say. Just because I wear a uniform—"

Tyler: "Well, some things go just beyond the clothes you wear." (*I don't like interjecting. But I've been doing it a lot recently.*) "Not saying people aren't superficial: they most certainly are. But there's more to a symbol."

Rollie: "And I get that. I do." (*He takes a pause. The eyes are small, but so are the lips and nose. Q. said it's like they shrunk his face altogether. I'm aware he's staring at me writing while my phone recording timer is clicking away the seconds on the bar. He steals a side-eye at Q. feet away, rolling wet drink glasses into his everything towel with his thumb and forefinger. Certainly eavesdropping...*)

The blinds are drawn in the office, obscuring the oncoming nighttime view. It had been a dry and gray couple of days, days in which the wind whisks by the corners of everything in an effort to announce the arrival of winter. Of course, the South Texas winter comes about like a forced palm upon the land, sudden and rigorous with its grasp. The sky acquiesces and yields an opaque pattern over its dominion. The traffic becomes nearly doubled with holiday shoppers and travelers, the spirits knocking around the guts of cars escaping through the tail end. Power lines are slackened yet more pronounced underneath the weight of migratory birds clinging to them with secure talons. The gray clouds pregnant with gloom explode in blackness as the birds scatter after some blaring traffic sound. Tyler hears the faint cawing outside, just underneath the whirring of a vacuum cleaner in another room.

He reclined in his chair and said to himself, "I wanted to hate you."

No longer staring at the notes, Tyler concerned himself with the screen empty of the article he wanted to write. There is scarcely a form that will perfectly fit to an idea—this is the curse with which the economy of consciousness must contest. The contention was form: how to address what needed to be said in such a medium. He deliberated the *how* of his work, *how* to stir his readers into caring about the things he cared about. Lurking somewhere in this deliberation stalked an ominous presence. There was an invisible, or rather a formless, foe in the midst of things. This enemy cast a hefty hand into Tyler's work, making things more complicated than he could presently handle. The recording, the notes—they were all there. He picked up the notes, set them down, unlocked his phone, let it time-out; returned to the notes; rested his hands before the keyboard, confronted the enemy on the screen; returned to the notes.

He took a deep breath of air that ran stray ribbons of sweet-smelling pan dulce into his mind.

Still reclined in his chair, Tyler lifted his gaze from the screen and above his cubicle, into a dark pocket of the office. There in that darkness not dissimilar to consciousness, he discerned the folds of velvet curtains bunching together to reveal the interior: the Tequila Worm; time: yesterday afternoon, when the only patrons at the bar consisted of himself, Tyler, and Rolando Flores. Quintanilla facilitated this meeting, being the owner of the bar and having a sweeping knowledge of Tiempo's populace. Those who operate a cantina haphazardly network through booze. Over three decades, Quintanilla has hosted personages of various echelons of power: mayors, congresspeople, musicians, athletes, punks, and he has occasionally given a pint to a number of homeless people in exchange for light work when he needed the help.

Quintanilla has never shied away from the press. Framed intermittently along the walls of the Worm are newspaper clippings depicting images of him shaking hands with prestigious guests. Eagle writers always authored these articles favorably, using phrases such as "historic bar" to describe Quintanilla's establishment, to which Quintanilla, himself, winced with a concealed pride. When Tyler requested the meeting between him and a young Border Patrol agent be arranged, Quintanilla seized the opportunity. "I'm doing this because you have looked out for Luis, *mijo*," he told Tyler after Rolando had called the bar to confirm the interview. "I don't like him much, but he seems to be an easy one to talk to. I'm not sure what's so important about a conversation like this. But remember to put my full name in there, *por favor*."

And so they sat, as Quintanilla feigned occupation.

(*He still avoids eye contact.*)

Tyler: "If we could talk about this story—"

Here, the notes take a break, as another patron enters the establishment, but from a door located adjacent to the bar that opens into the kitchen. The men turn their attention to the intruder: a brown narrow face frozen-over with eyes wide open, irises darting from the two guests to Quintanilla, the latter slowly roused to toss the cleaning towel over his shoulder and approach the young man with a sigh. The recording caught the sigh, along with the shuffling of Quintanilla's shoes across the back of the bar. Before the two disappear following the creaking of the kitchen door, Rollie's voice interrupts the scene.

Rollie: "Howdy, there. First time seeing you here."

There is no audible response from any party.

Tyler: "If I could get you back on this story, please." There is a harriedness to the young man's voice.

Rollie: "I hate coming to bars, especially old haunts like these. You could smell the years of cigarette smoke in the wood. Always hated the smell. Reminds me of what my old admiral used to say. He was this great North Texan bear of a man, white as a marshmallow, probably as bald, too. Tough sonuvabitch, but also, at similar measure—which is something he'd say all the time, the measure of things—he was equally as smart as all hell. You'd listen to him talk with people in other oversea outfits in different languages. He'd describe to you the components of things, especially the tools of war. He probably knew every battle that was ever waged. Told it to you as if he were there to witness it." (*He stares ahead of him into the mirror behind the bar. Slight smile lifting his cheek. Something of awe in his expression and the words he issues.*) "He told me once, Son, don't let the pride of man fool you; said, The greatest invention at man's hands is fire, for it is an illuminating force, but it is also a force of great destruction. Fire is the test of man's powers, he said. The smell of smoke upon the sea, billowing on the shores—that is the negative result of man's labor." (*He looks at the bar as if just discovering his fingers drumming on the cherry wood.*) "I always hated that man. Reminded me of how inadequate my father was. You contrast someone who seemed like he was culled from some ancient Texan winter with a lazy pedestrian of a person. His whole life pedestrian. Works all day for little money to put it into packs of cigarettes and the occasional family meal; sits out in his rundown truck smoking in the dark. He never left the Valley. I did the first chance I got. And when I came back…" (*Q. reenters the scene. The two men lock eyes. A biding moment compressed with unsaid words. There is a layer of disinterest veiled over a look of disdain on Q's face.*)

Rollie: (*When he speaks, he now raises his voice as if from a crowd.*) "You know, when you come back, there are certain expectations people put on you. This goes back to your symbol stuff." (*He tapped on my notes. Annoying.*) "The familiar faces you grew up with inspect you with great scrutiny, sensing a difference in you because they see the shine and the colors. They expect some sort of greatness in that uniform, like you've come from faraway lands defeating evil with a sword or something; and after all the celebration is done with, you're here to bring about a change within the confines of your hometown. I can't speak for every veteran. We all go through different struggles. Some seek some form of worship to alleviate that struggle, be it advocacy, drugs, the arts"—(*He scoffs at this.*)—"and some want to put their training into practice. Apply it to a heroic task of some sort."

Tyler: "Heroic task?"

Rollie: "Wouldn't you say keeping criminals at bay is heroic?" (*There's a smirk again. Air of owning the libs. Is he playing around with me?*) "You know, a lot of the older people I work with have this glazed look over their faces, a sort of resignation. I always chalked that down to years of experience, that oncoming boredom I soon must be facing, I guess. It took me a while before I realized that that look might be coming from a different place."

Tyler: "How so?"

Rollie: "Let's say we have these people who love doing the job in its various forms. I don't mean that they're in love with the career aspect of it—I mean that they see this job as an opportunity for them to, let's say, practice their moral conviction. There are bad guys out there. There's evil afoot. The measure of good is its opposition to evil. I've seen *güeros* handle them with more force than what you might think is necessary. The kicker is that our own people use an equal amount of force.”

Tyler: “That isn’t hard to imagine. With the lack of oversight, you all operate in this state-sanctioned Wild West.”

Rollie: (*Seeming to think about what I just said. His small eyebrows heighten.*) “You know, that’s not half bad.” (*Pause. Sound of 18-wheelers outside. Hissing breaks.*) “I haven’t been in the game for that long, and still… I’ve gotten the sense that our job has changed with every swinging dick in the White House, but even then…” (*He turned in my direction, starting and stopping himself. I glanced at a confused Q.*) “And so, on the day they had us dislodge that body from that buoy, there was an air of absurdity in it all.”

Tyler: “How do you mean ‘absurdity’? What was absurd about it, to you?”

Rollie: “Well, I guess the biggest, physical object is this long orange thing resting like a snake near the river bank. It’s weird to see something like that in the middle of a river of all places. You see those in larger bodies of water. And yet here we were, trekking through the water with reporters on our backs excavating the remains of a woman, the body all bloated, hair all over the place. We were just in charge of taking her out. We later found out she wasn’t even Mexican. It didn’t matter where she was from. Or maybe it does. But she wound up here. If you believe some of the stories in the media, they’re allegedly fleeing persecution, some threat of violence, death.”

Tyler: “And what do you think about those stories?”

Rollie: "Let's put it this way: There are lots of people, colleagues of mine, who weep over this shit. But we see it day-in, day-out. I've seen and heard of those who get shook by these stories, as well as the actual thing of it. They might've wanted to set out to do something about it. Y'know, cause some sort of ruckus on the inside. But what good would it do? This is a business, in fact. You'd be messing with someone's bottom line."

Tyler: "So you need someone to *pay you*—"

Rollie: "Look, all of this is fucked. From both sides of the traffic. What do people expect?" (*He looked me straight in the eye.*) "What do you expect from me? I don't relish this. You'd have to be some type of monster—"

Tyler: "Then why must you continue?"

Rollie: "Because it's a good living. I have friends in the agency. They are good people. I've heard the slogan 'All cops are bastards.' I assume that applies to people like me. Chase the institution, not me."

Tyler: "But you're a part of the institution."

Rollie: "I don't know what to tell you."

The recording trailed off into parting words. Tyler had let it run for a while after; he was now listening to the silent contours of the bar sighing a low frequency breath amid muted traffic sounds. There was less than a minute left on the recording. He remembered skimming the notes he had just taken, feigning interest in what was written over what he had just heard.

Having provided an orb of light around his person, the computer screen timed-out, abandoning Tyler in the now-emptied office. Babs, the Eagle janitor of over ten years, had left under an hour ago. He had heard the door shudder close and the minute rigidity of a worn key fitting and extricating from the lock across from where he sat. He wondered if she noticed he was still there. He shook his head. Of course, she knew; just as she knows he has a copy of the key. He had also heard her start her F-150 and peel out onto Main.

He made no move to stir the mouse and wake the monitor. A split-second before the recording on his phone finished, a rank smell of what could only be described as burning *marranitos* infiltrated the air.

At the end of the recording, Quintanilla asks Tyler, "Is that it?" as Tyler winces at the smell emanating from a ghost oven.

| * |

Night clouds clumped together overhead on the ride home. Their aggregate bore so low upon the land that the electric poles threatened to pierce the misty cumulonimbus, unleashing rain instantaneously.

Tyler drove his mother's car, brand new when she purchased it years ago. The upholstery at the center of the ceiling sank; the rubber grip on the steering wheel began to peel and leave residue on his hands; he could hear the rubber guard at the front of the car scrape gravel that knocked on the underside, miniscule but manifold. Even the aux cord, which his mother had dismissed as superfluous compared to her beloved collection of CDs she kept in the glove compartment, above title and registration, had to be cracked like a safe. Twist too far to one side and Tyler began cursing. There was a sweet spot that didn't involve static.

There remained another ten minutes before he would arrive home panning through nighttime traffic on Main bursting with Christmas displays and the uniformity of brake/head/traffic lights. (Yes, it is true, the traffic lights all down Main changed together. There was a window in which you could roll through half a mile without applying the brakes.) Tyler was stalled at a full-minute red light. He switched the audio on his phone connected to the delicate aux input to a recording he had taken after the interview with the border patrol agent.

In the cabin of his car, he could hear the whistling wind muffled and small and undulating over the layer of real-time wind brushing past soft and open. The sound carried him past the turn of the green light.

There is a patio area located in the rear of the Tequila Worm. This space Quintanilla reserved for his employees to take breaks and the occasional concert. Because of the tight dimensions of this area, every concert hosted behind the bar felt intimate—all but the first and last show led by the local band Sin Cacahuates, in which all four members of the band encouraged the audience to "fuck the establishment," resulting in a wave of electric vindication that soared like reverb across bodies turning over tables and cycling to form a pit chugging to sludge riffs and double pedals.

"Man, those ladies knew how to fuck shit up," Luis Ruiz said. His voice, as narrow as the rest of his body, perhaps twice as sharp, rose from the recording. Listening back in this way, he reminded Tyler of his dad's cousins, the ones living out on Boca Chica beach, and how quickly they talked. They hardly ever visited, but he remembered their presence as a child; his dad always telling them to repeat themselves because he couldn't keep up; his dad muttering under his breath, "It's because I'm not of blood"; him wising up to what they were doing and tuned them out with his accordion-playing outside under the shade of a mesquite orbited by beer cans emptied and crushed. They treated Tyler like a welcomed orphan in this way. He was the new baby to be celebrated, despite his father.

The memory lasted but a second as Tyler caught himself smiling in the faint reflection of the driver seat window turning off Main.

"You think your uncle would ever have them back?" Tyler asked Luis in the recording.

"No, sir," Luis replied immediately. "I love the man, but he is behind in the times when it comes to music and art and, pues, everything important."

"I see. Speaking of which, I wanted you to meet my friend here. This is Adrian."

"Sup." Another voice joined the recording, soft and short.

"She's been doing some weird stuff with her laptop and an

accordion."

"Weird?"

"I can see that. I haven't seen a setup like this ever," Luis admitted.

"I'll take that as a compliment, I guess."

"I wanted Luis to meet you. He likes to sing, and I know that you're in need of a vocalist."

"This is true. I hate hearing my voice on the songs I make. My Spanish isn't great, either, I'm afraid. I don't want to sound like an asshole, you know?"

"No yeah, I get it," Luis said. "Why don't you play something for us, and I can see if I can sing along, if that's alright."

"Sure, sure. I have the lyrics on my phone. I'll play it a couple of times, give you the model, then jump in when you want. Good?"

"*Dale.*"

For smart phone quality, the production sounded decent. Tyler heard Adrian click play on a program in her computer that set off a loop of harsh, glittery noise he hadn't heard before Adrian sent him a rough file on social media. He could see Luis draw back in astonishment as the noise burst through momentarily, shortly fizzing out for low ambience—and it was here that Adrian picked up her purple Hohner accordion, busy with stickers, holding one chord with fingers stretching across buttons the size and color of every wisdom tooth ever pulled, letting the billows breathe this one chord; the billows, too, stretching, revealing the velvet innards readying for exercise. Before long, and in time for a drum loop and synth accompaniment, Adrian caught the now-sagging bottom of the Hohner with her free hand and began playing low notes.

She closed her eyes when she sang. Quiet and stammering on lines she wrote, she didn't catch Tyler and Luis exchanging glances at each other. Adrian had given her phone to Luis, who bobbed his head to the bass-snare, so he could follow the lyrics, initially unsure that the noise coming from the laptop and Adrian's playing were the same song; but Luis caught the chorus which Adrian repeated twice, so that on the third utterance, Luis was already mouthing the words, "*No tengo pinche* money / Can't get no Valley Honeys / Cuz I'm short and ugly / *Pero mi mano* loves me." The track came to a close, and Adrian finally opened her eyes.

"And that's how it goes."

"You see how it's weird?" Tyler said to Luis.

"No, yeah. It's not like a *cumbia*, and it's kinda like rap; but like rap from the farm or something."

Adrian looked displeased. "So, you wanna try it or not?"

"No, no, it's *good*. It's *different. Vamos*."

The crash of noise that on second listen Tyler could feel the clashing of disparate parts resurfacing, to which Luis tapped his foot in order to preemptively frame the beat that was to come. He felt it then and before; and Tyler still felt something visceral about the combination of sounds that typically wouldn't land on the same track. Adrian played with familiar elements, but in such a way that it felt haphazardous, stupid, innocent. Tyler called this the purity of heart; and as he applied the brakes to park at his lonesome house, rain eking from the abundant dark mass above, he thought to himself how simple it would be to live in the velvet guts of that radical accordion.

When the song ended the second time, Adrian told her companions, "I wrote the lyrics to the song after a shift. Fuck a gas station, bro, I swear. No girls look at you."

"You sing this song to them, and it'll be a different story," Tyler said, imagining himself as a big-time artist or producer and they were having this conversation in a limo.

"Yeah, well, the music makes it better," Adrian responded.

"No, but better pay would be better. No?" Luis said, almost to himself, as he scanned the lyrics.

"We can't have everything," Adrian said, woebegone.

"*Y vamos*?"

Just this question from Luis and Adrian had already counted down for the track to restart. Tyler noticed how serious Luis had been during the session, how striking his features were as he sang the lyrics. "Look at him," Tyler said over the noise, "the definition—of an eagle!"

It was halfway through the jam that Tyler noticed a shadow leaning behind the party, in the tight alleyway letting out into the street. It was that last chorus in which the air drained from the recording, as the shadow inhaled to laugh.

Tyler yanked the aux cord from his phone and texted Luis,

then Q. He was gazing at the stout black windows of his house and clung to his phone for a response—anyone.

FATHER'S HAND:
TYLER LUCIO'S PAST AND PRESENT
SEEM AS ONE

Save for the aluminum roof, which persisted in bending where a felled tree branch put a dent into it years ago, the house stout and having already dug its heels into the dirt sat in the purple and open nighttime churning in the motions of winter, not quite shaking the entirety of the outside world, but making every particle from the dry, skeletal *espinas* tumbling about the grass to the slapping mesquite trees tremble in a slow ceaselessness that without sight amounted to static in Tyler Lucio's brain. That's what the Wall sounded like at his lonesome desk adjacent to a barred window curtained by a long, red towel. He had pinned a lower corner of the towel to the side with a lamp, staring into the black triangle of the outside world hurling soft, disintegrating palms across the glass.

With a dubious eye, he turned his attention to the laptop screen threatening to time-out by dimming its brightness. He was quick to pass a finger over the trackpad. Wake up, computer!—followed by a neck roll, followed by a dispirited spin in the swivel chair, a quick scan of the bedroom…

- Immediately to the right of the desk, an entertainment center void of a television, and in its stead a lean regiment of books at ease, leaning on one after the other;
- before the small library, a twin bed occupies a little under half of the room, cutting across the chipping and swollen linoleum with a bulbous comforter mounded to the side, waiting for Tyler's retirement;
- the doorway ajar and itself another portal but to other rooms of the mobile home running like cable cars, themselves unstirred, dim, the gas oven in the kitchen cracked ever-so-slightly at a low temperature, glazing every article of the interior with a light slime, the heat just barely shoring up to Tyler's silent figure, but the scent of propane omnipresent and slightly nauseating;
- on the purple wall to the right of the doorway, a framed

picture of his mother, pregnant with Tyler, standing beneath whatever shade a sunhat could afford amid the harsh sun and the frozen waves about to crash and the drowned and darkened sand, her rounded almond belly protruding from the end of a Dr. Pepper shirt;

- beneath this frame a short dresser and, resting atop without breath but all pearl and shimmer, a Gabbanelli accordion sitting tight-lipped, the music in its guts stifled from years of inaction, this the last image watching from across the room as the chair's rotation stopped like a roulette wheel at the desk, the dimming computer, the Wall.

Confrontations with the Wall occurred with increasing frequency, now that his father switched his sunken bed, located at the opposite end of the house, with a stiff hospital gurney, his own room that used to know a woman's touch for a sterilized and staid room whose atmosphere burdens like weight you never planned on bearing.

'Nothing is ever planned,' Tyler thought, tapping the backspace key on a blank sheet. He wrote chapters in separate documents. He felt it was clean that way: Other chapters were not lurking above or below, distracting him. Off to the side of the desk, next to his computer, a yellow legal pad laid bare the outline for his novel. Currently, the plot is eluding him. How do you type the next word if you don't know where you're going? One may seek instruction from their masters…

He had taken a few semesters of English courses in Edinburg before he would have to call it quits for his dad and a full-time job. ("Every adult pushed a degree on us growing up, but nowadays you need to go to grad school in order to get anywhere," he reasoned to his friends at the time. "Then to get into debt the further along I get. When does it end?") Glancing at his books, most of which he had accumulated during his undergrad years, he realized how sick he was of his favorite writers. He had read how culture had mythologized nineteenth-century greats—authors like Herman Melville, Walt Whitman, and Emily Dickinson—as these lonesome figures, alienated from the rest of the country, the rest of the world. Loneliness seemed to be the center of greatness, of success. He knew better, though. He knew none of these writers cloistered themselves; there was an American literary legacy of being about the world, bearing witness and engaging with people, movements, and ideas that informed their work. Still, mythology and myth-making are sturdy structures. He *desired* them so. The hermeneutics in the pursuit of art, no matter how incomplete that may be, tempted him in its aesthetics. What's more, it made the arrival of a hero that much more inevitable; that is to say, in the formless and germinating non-mass that is his book, he waited for a singular figure to emerge, bearing in their advent the impetus for change, and thus inspiring him to write thousands of words because it would all make sense. If only one fictive person could do that.

As if his fantasy for a hero wasn't imperiled by the reality of authorial biographies, Américo Paredes drove a spike into his conscience at the end of *George Washington Gómez*. Where was the hero at the end of that story? Did the War end heroism, or was there ever such a thing before the mass killing across the Atlantic? Did the bomb erase the chance for Chicanx leadership? Faces of his friends rotated in his mind like a neurotic carousel, all of them grappling with their experiences in the world, in America, in the Rio Grande Valley—in Tiempo. Willie's eyes were downcast, so that twin shadowy pits sat under his eyebrows, averting the scrutinizing gaze of his parents who still believed that homosexuals would be stoned if not in the present life, then the next. Then the narrow dark face… Diego's pronounced smirk could scarcely lift him from memories of classmates making fun of his imitation brands his mom would score at *la pulga*, simultaneously scrutinizing how his English was underdeveloped compared to his Spanish. Then the narrow dark face shoring up… Flor's unrelenting teeth gritting in pain from the grip her man sustained over her with furious undefeat against the agents of class warfare, the latter of which recommended hard work and distrust toward his colleagues, himself maintaining the opinion that a man must provide for the household, even if the house held him beneath its crushing cinder blocks and bills.

Then the narrow dark face shoring up, unblinking, dire, nostrils flared, desperate for air—

A gray matter began lining the floors along all four corners of the mobile home.

Out of focus behind the face the sound of waves in a low ceaseless rhythm; the muted grackles aloft in the night, the darkness of their breast gradients darker than the subconscious—

The gray matter rose to fit around each item of the house, from doorstop to ceiling fan, leaning on Tyler's back like a dumb animal awaiting acknowledgement. The black triangle of the window transfixed him. He wasn't staring at it, that's just where his mind resided for the moment.

Then the narrow dark face swung direction at the sound of a struggle in the water—

Now gelatinous in body, the gray matter opened its fist and enveloped Tyler.

| * |

Weatherman Tim Smith forecasted a windy night "and probably more to come." Tyler could hear the night working its tirade among the chain link fences and the dead trees. Sounding like it would rip the roof from the house, it also caused the aluminum above him to flex and belch like thunder.

Although the branch—which wasn't just a branch, but once felled tore down and essentially quartered the jacaranda whose purple trumpet flowers were extinct now for, well, memory does not recollect for how long, but sometimes their purple ghosts levitate behind the eyes and high in the naked limbs—although this branch had snapped years ago, and nothing lingered over that particular corner of the roof that bent and warbled that night or a manifold of

132

nights previous, something snapped overhead, once more, which finally left the screen idle enough to blink. The screen be damned: Tyler focused on the black triangle in the background, formed by the pinned-back blanket and the window, whose security bars were uniform with the nighttime darkness. The ghost branch of the mesquite adjacent to his room succumbed to—

Memory takes him back to a time before his father discovered his sickness—even before Tyler's mother suffered from the heart disease that felled her the year Tyler turned sixteen.

The whirring wintry wind blowing away at his window transforms his surroundings to those of a car, at a moment when he and his mother cut through midnight on a lonesome expressway. At the time of this memory, his mother, a woman of forty who had not the fear or thought of her heart conditions that would take her life a year later, had just finished her night shift at a restaurant. Although no longer at the restaurant, her employer had tasked her with delivering parcels to another branch located in McAllen. Knowing her teenage son would be awake (due to the numerous nights she came home to find the bottom of his door pulsating with television light), and with a heavy yet faint subconscious consideration that suggested to her that the twelve-hour shifts might have taken something intricate and imperative away from their relationship, Tyler's mother promptly drove home, picked her son up, and started for the expressway without any noticeable objections.

Everything comes in bursts of light, streaks across the car

window, shrinks, and disappears steadily from existence, each lamppost a new addition to the road's ellipses. Outside the world is cold, almost overwhelmingly dark, yet with a punctuating sense of life. In the passenger seat, Tyler places his hand to the window and feels the delicate, exhilarating shock of the outside world. He can't imagine himself existing out there in that mix-up of coldness, darkness, and light that thrived and vanished in one breath. He can't imagine it, but he does recognize a faint image of a boy with similar physiognomy outside the window staring into the car with timid, searching eyes.

"So, how's your writing coming along, Ty?"

The voice shakes him through memory like a hand grasping his shoulder, this being the effect of his recollection that suspends him somewhere between in the car and outside of it: the window. Inside the car, however, Tyler's younger self turns to his mother unabashedly, the Tyler outside of memory jealous of the boy.

"It's coming along," he replies. He has heard other writers talk about their work in interviews on C-SPAN, his consumption of which he has kept from his friends because American teenagers were more readily attuned to reality television and the language of the partygoer, not the quiet library talk about the praxis of literary theory or the opining on the decadence of American culture.

His mother smiles ahead of her, her big honeysuckle eyes shortly invisible to him, the white skin of her face orange and dark under light and non-light. Her short, dark hair fits around her head, hiding her thoughts from the world. To her son, she seems ambiguous yet known, known to be his mother, known to care and provide and nurture and love the best she can, working two to three jobs; but ambiguous in the sense that the boy hardly ever saw or spoke to her since the age of five.

"You know, once you get it published and before everyone in the world starts talking about it, I want to be one of the first to read it." Once she says it, she turns to him; and when she does this, a passing lamppost of orange light peeks inside the car to reveal her eyes: bursting with a sun's reflection; something cosmic; something boundless; wondrous, unambiguous, small: It is like looking at the big picture through two little frames; with a presence minute, yet with an impression of infinitude. She returns her physical attention to the road. She asks, "Do you know what it's going to be about?"

Staring off into the vast expanse of world, Tyler's words transmit slowly—"I want to write about people. I'm interested in them the most."—he settled himself in the seat—"I can't imagine anything more interesting."

"That seems like a huge topic, don't you think?"

Tyler nods.

"Well, if you believe you can do it, then so do I."

A minute, twinkling dewdrop of warmth leaks through memory into knowing, the feeling transcendent through time. But the teenager doesn't miss her yet, so he smiles a confused smile and leaves an open ellipsis.

Tyler, the boy who would graduate high school in six months, waits outside the heavy wooden doors of a church. He waits without impatience, yet there looms something over him, something the church and all its earthly power can't quell. It surrounds him, its stifling breath clean and stale like the exhumed body of an angel. Even though a beacon of faith and quite often the opportune place for unburdening oneself—and Tyler notices how almost everyone leaves with light steps, the Lord's anointed—it does nothing for the boy waiting by the exit. He doesn't seek it. He doesn't seek at all.

'He's sick, Mom. I wish I could tell you. I wish I could talk to you about it as we would in the car. I wish I could with you because I can't with him. It's so hard to talk to him. Look at them having an easy time with words, talking amongst themselves in huge groups, all half faces turned to each other. I couldn't stay never liked those kneelers. Repentance starts at the Amá. And it's not only because he suddenly needs God. Please. It's so hard to talk to people who have their eyes set on *not dying*.

'He thinks any of this will save him. Chances are he'll live and give all the credit to God and none to the doctors who don't know what the fuck they're doing. All they know is bad news and paychecks. Fuck, now I sound like him. What's taking him…

'But if he does… Who's gonna mourn his death? Who'll show up to his funeral? The family across the river don't care much for him, and the ones here—well, whoever's left here… I'm actually not sure who remains of the Lucios after Grandma. All that history is gone, practically. And as for friends… He *had* friends, just ones I remember seeing as a child when he used to play shows and take mom and me with him, then eventually just me in a weird affectation, some sort of bid against Mom. He was proud those days. They looked at him and his musical genius and saw a kind of cultural hero that made them hold their partners close, spinning and shifting along the hardwood. Little did they know that that life didn't pay so well when you had a kid, much less when you opened multiple lines of credit all across town. He was proud to pay those bills, though. Didn't matter if he had to take the loss and get an actual nine-to-five and settle for the random gig. He was still proud. Immensely venomous. But proud. Now it's all pathetic.

'Ah, great. Now he has a congregation following him out. We don't need all of this attention.

'What can they do anyway? All they can do is say some prayers off some beads and wishes because that's how you gain access to heaven when you're dead, or *dying*: You have others convince the Decider that you're not such an asshole. And they'll tell me that he's going to a better place. *They* are going to tell me that *he's* going to a better place. Would they say that for *you?* He still holds that against you against me. And they'll say that. He works in mysterious ways. And that's all they're concerned about Him and his mysterious ways. Death isn't mysterious. Everyone has Him on their mind when someone dies I couldn't. I can't. When you died, I couldn't think of Him at all.'

From his position at the bottom of a set of wide marble steps that close inward to the tall wooden doors of the church, Tyler witnesses his father.

'He's a lot slower now. I don't know if it's something he's putting on, some performance he decided would get people to feel sorry for him. He's always concerned about how other people see him.

'Look at him. At the center of attention, with all those people with their eyes closed and their hands raised and even the fucking priest locking his hands on his shoulders saying prayers at a hundred miles an hour.'

Legs unsteady under the manifold tongues vying for ordained endurance, Felix Maldonado's knees caught his fall, soliciting the concern of churchgoers nearby, while one whose attention was before spellbound suddenly turned away, down the stone walkway, onto a bright and bleak autumn afternoon: an unbroken sheet of cloud with no sun. The trees stand naked, petrified, and gray, as if drawn to reality by charcoal. Huddling birds cling to the branches absent of leaves.

Abrupt clanging from high up the bell tower smoothed the land below in sweeping, repetitious pangs. Another heated bilingual sermon awaits everyone inside, the strictly Spanish-only sermons reserved for the early, *early* hours and the late, *late* ones. (The English-only sermons held at some church no one in the crowd ever heard of.)

'Cowboy hats and large, elaborate belt buckles; stiff ironed shirts undoubtedly ironed this morning in the early darkness. Their shirts are tucked in, for the most part, even those whose paunches test the limits of cotton. Jerseys, jerseys—are the Cowboys doing good this season? Long dresses, oversized blouses, stuff you know their sister or mother wore a time ago; blue jeans that run just above the heel. They rub their hands like they're trying to iron out a knot deep in the palm. I can almost see their fingerprints on a callous layer. They steal glances at the young ones; they're staring at the boys and following their stares at the girls who're risking heaven and taste by wearing low-cut blouses, short jean shorts, and cowboy boots. The moms wanna say something to them, but they'll settle with silently reproaching them with their eyes that switch from coldness to sincerity without much thought, like the clicking of a machine. They're all quite concerned for each other, not really for themselves—and all of their thoughts remain hidden underneath tamed hair, cowboy hats, and noncommittal gazes. Their eyes are darting around—how am I so different—each target needs to be scrutinized—how am I so different—beckons the silent snares of reading—how am I so different—because speech is mythical on the pathway to God.

'They're on me now. I can feel it. A wall of eyes like a collective surveillance creeping up behind me, wrapping around me. The trees sound like static. I—'

A soft hand—a hand that hardly ever saw rough manual labor from years of working at the local Tiempo Regional—a hand that glided across smooth buttons on an accordion—rested on Tyler's shoulder. It seems fresh as if right from creation. The other hand remains unformed, hidden in the shadow of Tyler's unseeing.

'You all knew it,' he thinks, 'You all saw it before I did.'

He became absent in his recollection, without form, rather. Instead, a rush of wind and a descending of grackles spun his formless essence until he was nothing but periphery and mirror, reflecting the crowd around him, the woebegone faces crushed with sympathy but strung together by the gaze.

Even in recollection, the thoughts are whispers: 'What if I shrug it off? Would it matter to you?

'Of course I'm gonna help him down the goddamn steps. What should it matter to you? You're not my family. You're not family at all. The only thing that ties you all together is looking. It's me, and it's him, and it's you looking at us like it's something to look at, like you're just waiting to see if things go exactly in order.

'What should it matter to you?' *What should it matter to you*

Out of the church and back into the immediate reality, Tyler is split in two. While one Tyler remains transfixed on the black triangle, the other with narrowing eyebrows swivels slowly toward the doorway of his room, down the short hall that leads into the living room. There in that unlit domain, voices of ghosts made perpetual by Tyler's knowing manifest through an escalating reel of sound.

well he inst mine is he

please dont say that around him its already enough that you still think like that

still think like what

i just wanted you to take him to school i have a shift in an hour

right i always have to bend over backwards for you i have work in the morning too you know i didnt sign up for this

then why did you come crawling back huh you couldve stayed practically homeless playing at shitty bars getting nowhere with your friends i didnt have to take you back in

i dont do it for the money

thats for sure thats why youre deep in the shit and you asked me to help bail you out

i dont have anything you understand i thought playing would get me somewhere i thought i could do something with it i thought i was important now its all left me do you know what it feels like to chase something to want something greater than you are right now

i do and hes in the other room right now

thats not my kid why couldnt you just lie to me and tyler of all names

you think possession makes you a man huh

you dumb bitch i have nothing to my name

get out of the way ill take him to school suns not even out yet and youre drunk its not a good look anymore you know all your friends are dying early theyre dying listening to the old songs you play why dont you try something new for once

i have nothing no one follows me anymore

i know things were different back then when everyone wanted a change its sad that it seems like they dont want it anymore

i had them

maybe you did one time but they all walked away im asking for you to see your son hes yours

but he doesnt want to learn how to play

maybe thats not for him

i dont have to be here

you really dont now make some coffee i gotta call work to tell them im gonna be late clean yourself up

"Just please, stop…"

Tyler clasps his head with both hands as if trying to stifle the memory. Air rushes through his nostrils, the color of his face reddening. After a few breaths, his grasp lessens, eyes ease shut, face slowly returns to normal color, though he could feel a vein at the top of his forehead throbbing like a tiny heart attempting to escape. 'All in a little vein,' he thinks and repeats 'vein' in his head. Immediately following this moment of collection, his eyebrows narrow, the vein kicks. Once again, the reel starts.

—"Look at the birds."

Back at the church.

His father speaks behind him, a voice without body but with weight.

"Look at the birds, mijo," his father repeats. "They look like crosses when they fly, don't they? The seasons are going by."

Tyler says through memory and mouths the words at his lonesome: "Crosses? Maybe. But I can't see why a bird would carry any weight like that."

The memory in image freezes: the people that surrounded him and his father as Tyler remembered them to look like; his father with that sagging face and the humble smile, arm extended; Tyler, himself, amiss.

| * |

The face swung back, like a stone dial stopping short across the night, from surveying the orange streetlight washing the pockmarked Alacran Circle to watching the figure pacing before a short count of steps leading up to the entrance of a mobile home. Angst fell upon Luis Ruiz's sharp face as he watched Tyler Lucio make bounded tracks beneath the dead jacaranda tree.

"Will you stop this? Your grass is already gone as it is," Luis said.

Tyler's head poked up.

"And why can't we go inside, bro? It's actually cold outside."

Their arms were folded across their chests, burying their knuckles into their armpits.

"I just don't wanna be in there right now," Tyler replied, continuing his pacing.

"I would've brought my Tio's jacket if I knew we'd be outside like this." Wind rushed past Luis's face, blowing his short, dark hair back. His eyes began to dry and well. "Look, bro, all of what you said is kinda bad, I get it. But you can't stay locked in these memories."

"I feel like I can't help it. I thought out of everyone, you would understand…"

"Don't misunderstand *me*. Look, I think about that night all the time. You could even say I'm living that night over and over. But I can't stop. She wouldn't want me to. You don't think yours would say something, or maybe even smack some sense into you."

"She never laid a finger on me. A lot of my classmates when we were small talked about the *chancla* and the pinpoint accuracy of their mothers' aims; but I never saw that. We were always doing something, those days. She was really into gardening. Planting and growing—those were her things. In fact"—his steps paused—"she had to fight for this tree. She told me about it one day: how important this was to her; and not just this tree, which I can't tell you how long it's been dead; but the process of growing things, *making* things. She told me Dad had to cave because it meant to her what music meant to him; that somewhere deep there was a pain—and I'm not sure what or which pain she was talking about specifically—but that there was this pain deep inside the skin that needed to be healed; that while other people can come by and help you out with this pain, you had to turn within yourself and create something outward: to turn within yourself and cast outward, see? Sounds a little self-helpy. Sounds like she couldn't understand how everything is useless in the face of everything that's out to get you."

"It sounds to me like she knew more than all that. There *is* something in there. It's not what they say about being born into sin, like at church. It's something more… And I think she knew that just because you were busy healing yourself, it doesn't mean you have to stop other things. Like you said: within and out."

The wind no longer sounded like static, but eased into a low soughing that hummed around the objects of the outside world.

"I'm sure this tree was beautiful when it was full."

"Yeah, it really was." Tyler gazed upward at the open bowl of sky burning at the edges with city lights, gazed through skeletal branches. "No one's tended to it. I haven't seen those purple leaves in a long time."

"Can it be saved?"

The two locked eyes. An orange hue reflected off Luis's face still dim from the shadow of the chain link fence cordoning the front yard from the street. Half of Tyler's figure hid in the shadow of the jacaranda.

"Y'know, I'd rather just forget about the whole thing," Tyler said, turning his face so that now all of it was submerged in shadow.

Luis narrowed his eyes at Tyler, attempting to read an expression stolen from him.

"There are so many other things to worry about," Tyler continued. "I would rather forget and put more attention elsewhere."

Standing up and shivering, Luis responded, "I don't think that's it, either. But have it your way. I'm going inside before my *nalgas* fall off my butt."

THE DAY THEY TOOK HIM AWAY

That morning, he recalled a story his nephew told him one day about his mom, and how there are islands in the river where the two of them hid. It seemed like a fantasy now that he recalled it. Like a story you knew was impossible, yet the way his nephew told it made it concrete.

"It starts the way every escape starts," his nephew began, "the way all rivers begin—with rain—and then slowly courses through land to make it back to the sea."

He told this story on the second day of his arrival. He had piercing blue eyes, the kind that settle and bear upon you; and the way his body leaned toward you, his face tan and sharp, like the edge of a cliff, narrowed periphery; but his quizzical eyebrows and honest, direct speech disarmed.

The day he arrived, his uncle knew nothing of his journey. They were both in his house, and outside the cutting joy of children's laughter swam through the air, as it tends to do in the long days of summer that do not die until half of October is gone. Yet it is early winter, and the children kick around the volley/soccer ball with the clapping of *chanclas*. The windows are open. A strong breeze animates the beige curtains, golden by a good sun. It seems like the house breathes.

"Mama built a fire on the island. She said we would be okay. That the trees would shield the light. And she was right. We spent most of the evening there, unnoticed. It was like no one cared if we lived or died, as if no one knew we existed. It felt relieving, to be in that river on the sand, looking at the stars, listening to both the passing water that forked around us, and the sound of cars that sounded like cats purring by—but they seemed far away. They couldn't touch us.

"She told me a story about you, Tio. If you can believe it, Tio, she loves you very much, no matter what happened between you two—and I forget what that is or was. She told me about some time in the seventies, how Ama told both of you to draw water from the well. (I didn't know we had wells anymore, until that night.) She told me how Ama told her to help you draw the water because you couldn't reach the thing that drops and pulls the bucket."

His uncle nodded. "Yes, yes—the well in the ranch. Estrella—

your mom—used to tell me stories about how if you drop yourself into that well, you fall forever, never hitting bottom; and how it would get so dark once you fell, that the circle of light"—he made an "o" with his fingers—"would become a dot; and how after it disappears, the only light you will see is your memory of that circle that gets smaller and smaller.

"Even though she told me these things, she would pretend to push me down while clinging to my shirt. That would scare the shit out of me. But after she did that to me twice, I did not have to change my underwear anymore; it had become something like a thrill."

His nephew laughed and said, "She never mentioned that, Tio!"

Quintanilla got red in the face. He got red telling his nephew, Luis, something that embarrassed him, as if the man he is was far removed from the boy he was. He thought about that while reminiscing about his childhood on the ranch in Mexico his father owned at one time, and about his nephew's story.

It hadn't succeeded much over a fortnight since Quintanilla received a rapping on his door, him opening it and beholding the pink, twilight sky erupting from the ground and his nephew vertically stitching the two—his head and upper torso where Orion's Belt might have been, and the rest of his body over the Earth—his feet on Quintanilla's welcome mat. Quintanilla would recall his hesitation when ushering him into his home. Although many thoughts rushed through his conscience, what punctuated them were the memories of his sister and how they left things between them.

He remembered the look on Estrella's face when he left, the same look she gave him that summer when they had chased their mules with their father during a flooding rain. The mud-colored mules now grayer in the static curtains broke free from their stakes, dragging them along through the muddying crops. Their father had caught a straggler and, leading the huffing beast by the stake and rope, tasked Estrella with bringing it to where the cows were. Their mother was yelling something from the house. Estrella could scarcely see a few feet before her, trekking across the now-bowl of mud that was the dirt path between the house and the barn which stood like a dark mansion against the static rain. She could hear off in the distance her brother and father shouting out in the fields.

Inching closer to the barn, she saw the stone well overflowing. Through some trick of imagination and whatever moon lingering above the world that night dropping silver coins generously across the land, Estrella discerned debris turning in the well. Fastening the rope around her fist and drawing the mule's head closer to her, so that the animal's dumb eye bore witness, too, the girl felt the ground give as the debris in the well transformed from sticks to bones to sticks again. She found footing again and entered the dark barn with the mule in tow.

Sometime during their corralling, Alfredo had managed to apprehend one mule in the direction he went, knowing somewhere in the opposite direction his father was looking at five others.

Earlier, when the rain had just made landfall breaking from the crest of a distant mountain range, he stood by the front doorway, watching his father sitting in his bone-hard wicker, lighting his pipe. "Did you hear me?" Alfredo asked to a nearly absent reception. The oncoming rain swept over them, as if to shush him. He could see his sister through the window, clenching the parted curtain in the half-moonlight. The eyebrows were sharp enough to cut the shadow while the eyes pierced, unblinking. Her mouth was fastened shut. She chewed on her gums. She didn't need their father to utter a word for her to turn away.

By the time Alfredo repeated himself, his father grumbled as if stirred from slumber. Alfredo stared incredulously at the figure rising from the wicker; but before wasting another word, he heard the slosh-trot of six mules, jaunting almost in file past the porch.

"Bring your sister," his father ordered. Before he motioned to move, Alfredo saw the shadow of himself, of what the future held for him in dirtied pants and shirt that symbolized for him the wealth of the land, precisely how bankrupt it had made him and his family—he saw his father peer around the corner and leap into the downpour, which began to crescendo in his absence, leaving Alfredo stuck by the doorframe, not intending to run into the house to fetch Estrella, but fighting all desire to follow in the memory-trail of the escaped mules and skip over their dragging stakes and not stop in the confusion of the rain until it had all ran out of him.

His father returned from the side of the house leading a mule.

"Bring your sister so she can put this one away."

He, too, was the color of the mule with the rain pelting away at him, dabbing his open face slick and sharp, the grit of undefeat salient and annoying to his son. So, when Alfredo followed his father's voice cutting through miles of static and found three mules tied to his wrist, his hand gray in the wash, the opposite arm braced across his chest, he couldn't reconcile the two faces: the one half-flushed in the mud, the other left lingering before the porch.

Three taut ropes linked the animals to the man. Alfredo worked on unraveling his father's wrist, the stakes crisscrossed against the manacled hand that, once freed, remained frozen in place, grappling something that wasn't there. It reminded Alfredo of the head of the rake his father kept off the side of the barn.

Together, they were a four-legged creature, the one leaning on the other, pushing through the rain. Under the arm and closer to his father's chest than he has ever been and will ever be, Alfredo felt the stunted breathing rising in a short meter upon his cheek. It was a debilitation of which his father would not see the end until the grave years later, after his wife had already left him for another man, and all who was left was Estrella and her only son out of wedlock to bury him in the back of the house, away from the mountains and by the mules she would let free following an exhausting, tearless prayer.

| * |

Alfredo would leave his family's ranch in 1983, not without a sense of guilt from his sister, mother, and father. What he would take—the clothes on him, a gallon of water, and a suitcase containing a razor, papers, some money, a few changes of clothing, and a faux-ruby rosary his mother slipped inside amongst the other articles of the suitcase, doing so only after Alfredo left it lying about in the kitchen—all of this traveled with him over the Rio Grande and dozens of miles speckled with potholes into the new country.

It took all but a week of sleeping in cafes and downtown benches and church pews before Alfredo would land a flat in a city called Tiempo. It was a "shitty" flat, as the renter admitted. Emptying his jean pockets of everything that might be considered currency, Freddy felt a pang deep within him. "I don't have a family to send money to. So, these pesos are all I have," he reasoned with the landlord. The hand hesitated, as if repelled; but the landlord took the money-fold and flipped through it, his nostrils scrunching, smelling the sweaty pants off each bill. He wasn't counting, so much as looking Freddy over with shifty eyes. The both of them knew Freddy had more money on his person. It was a game for the landlord to guess where Freddy was hiding it. Could he tickle it out of him? "I'll use it the next time I cross the river," the renter said, before time became too conspicuous. He leafed a few bills from the fold and returned them to Freddy. "You take these. You'll need them; and besides, since these new ones came out, that Chacmool always gives me the creeps when I see it."

Having found a stable place to return, Freddy would take on various jobs around Tiempo, finding work in construction, the type of work not too removed from the farm labor he endured with his family, but novel enough to him that it challenged his muscle memory.

There was a quiet camaraderie amongst the workforce, many of whom traveled together in truck flatbeds, bouncing off potholes, holding onto caps and tools, not unsmiling. "I'm going to Houston one of these days," one would say to the derision of others. "You're still going to get paid the same, no?" another would respond. "There's more of us here, now," the first voice said. The man expressing his opinion surveyed the faces rounding the truck bed. "A lot of you are new," he continued, "all of you with visas for work." Freddy slowly felt for the paper through his jeans. "There will be enough of us going around here. I like the big cities. Who knows"—the man said this now gazing downwards at the center of the truck bed—"maybe they will pay me more up there." Most of the crew erupted with laughter. "Maybe they will pay you *there* like a *gringo* dishwasher *here!*" Similar conversations accompanied the troop every waking day, before the sun broke and spilled its golden yolk across all of Tiempo.

Meanwhile, Freddy saved most of his American dollar, stuffing the leaves of cash into a slit in his mattress a renter before him must have made...

"Those days were hard," Quintanilla admitted to his nephew, Luis Ruiz. He returned Luis's gaze as if climbing down a dream. He hadn't known for how long the memories of bygone days had stolen his attention.

It was now late afternoon, and the beige curtains had quit

billowing for some time and became dark, reflecting the overcast sky. Shuffling feet about the house—no doubt Beatrice busied with fixing accommodations for her nephew, of whom she had never met before this sobering day. She entered the *sala* and noticed the two sitting across from each other in dimness.

"I put your stuff in Lena's room and made the bed," Beatrice said, flipping the light switch.

"Speaking of which," Quintanilla continued, his countenance relieved from its forlorn connection with Luis, "that was about the time, more or less, when I met your Tia. Wasn't it?"

Signaled from rummaging through kitchen drawers, Beatrice rejoined the two, approaching Quintanilla from behind, standing and smoothing the throw blanket draped over the couch. Her hands never stopped.

"What, when we first met?" she asked.

"Yes, when I would go to your dad's bar after work. Of course, I didn't know it belonged to him…"

"Oh, of course you did!"

"No, I didn't! I should have known because the way you talked with everyone there, it made it seem like *you* owned the place. Isn't that right?"

"Well, I wasn't afraid of anyone."

"Yes, because your dad was always there. Watching. Like Washington on a dollar bill. Just watching, waiting for something to go wrong."

"And nothing ever did. Except you marrying me."

Luis could tell that turning around that quickly strained his uncle's neck by the wince he gave his wife.

"Tio."

Quintanilla carefully swiveled his neck, the wince on his lip still fixed on his face.

"The guy that helped me find you. He kept calling you by another name. Not Robles."

Quintanilla sat there, his lip easing into one straight line, the energy leaving his face completely. He felt a hand quietly roll over his shoulder, smoothing the fabric of his shirt.

| * |

The suburbs of Tiempo do not have their unique name, as other suburbs do. One finds that testing the membrane of Tiempo does not constitute exiting Tiempo proper. (This would require a full commitment.) So, when Freddy traversed the crumbling road leading to his father-in-law's house, a road once unblemished, he had no illusions that where he was driving, that his destination, was still in the boundaries of Tiempo, though the cityscape reeled behind the curve of the earth, biting the sky in its jagged geometry.

Beatrice's father had stopped coming to holiday gatherings or birthday celebrations a few years ago, but kept the image of him being alive by sending cards with a few bills attached. Not only was he still breathing in the world, but he also continued to perform an act of care.

Maintaining direction, Freddy's hands rubbed the now-spongy leather of the steering wheel, picked at its wearing surface. He didn't think he would have had to explain his surname change to anyone for the rest of his life, much less explain it to his sister's son. He didn't. He silently sat on his couch that afternoon a month ago and let Beatrice interject. She didn't explain anything, either. Instead, she proceeded to give her nephew a tour of the home. Neither of them explained anything—not that it mattered now.

He remembered meeting him—the old man, Beatrice's father—not too long after meeting Beatrice, in the same bar with a wooden sign swinging overhead the front doorway, reading, TEQUILA WORM. Although shorter than him, Beatrice's father sized Freddy up and down, holding his gaze with his chin jutted toward Freddy's face like a fleshy lance.

"So, it's you who my daughter's been running around with…"

"Yes, sir. It's nice to meet you. My name—"

"Answer me a few things, will you?" Freddy had already extended his hand. Not breaking eye contact, he withdrew into his pocket. "How did you get here?"

A crowd had just entered the bar, yammering its way to a table.

"I'm sorry, sir?"

"Where is your family?" The way he positioned his face underneath the bar light gave a bronze finish to the man.

Still quite unassuming, Freddy answered, "My family? They're in Mexico."

Unmoved, Beatrice's father replied, "Yes. What is your family's name?"

Every lingering second brought about the idea that within this conversation there was a game being played, of which he had entered handicapped. This suspicion notwithstanding, Freddy answered: "Robles."

A smirk wedged itself into the stone cheek of Freddy's interviewer. "Robles?" he said, not so much as a question, but in effect to turn it on his tongue. His eyes lifted and inspected some middle-space off and up in a dark pocket of the bar, the eyebrows lax as if entertained, finally, for the first time in years.

"We're a farming family," Freddy inputted, without as much conviction as its verity necessitated. It was as if he didn't believe it himself; that he came from such a family perhaps felt like an invention. Was this someone else's history?

"Robles?" the other repeated with greater intrigue. He at last leveled eye contact with Freddy. "That's all well and good. It shows great strength to come from humble beginnings. People around here love those stories. I come from horse trainers, myself. Of course,"—he raised his hands up before him—"I haven't seen work like that in what seems like a few decades."

The word "stories" stuck to the wall of Freddy's mind, how something for all his life revealed some sort of truth about the world and about the person telling the tale seemed trivialized by the man before him, the man whose powers he had to at the very least circumnavigate in order to gain a greater access to love in his daughter. This latter notion he needn't worry for much longer, as the older man ran a diatribe around Freddy's attention—about the *appearance* of things, the look of a family, perhaps the Robles's, who at the fore of their livelihoods understood the humility of the earth but, according to Beatrice's father, were forever on the sharp curve of the sickle. The word "ownership" began to surface.

"Something I foresee in our future"—and here, Freddy understood the "our" in this statement—"is the complete inability for us to own land. These are different times than when Roosy was president and little guys like us, like your parents, could own something that they could be proud of without being bought out by someone who, let us be honest, does not have their best interest in mind. Those who have nothing to begin with—well, they will be left in the dust. You have to own something of worth and acquire it and maintain it in such a way…" The older man strayed momentarily, then recouped in a lower register. "I didn't choose the name; and if you ask me, it reeks of Anglo. When they first came down and wanted to make the first *cantina*, I suppose they wanted to appeal to *us*. Or maybe it was a joke. Either way, I married into it…"

It took a year of courtship before Freddy would receive the offer. Maybe it was something about the times, the Cold War ethics of mistrusting identities, that enticed him to acquiesce; or maybe the distance he felt from a story, more specifically a void of communication to another life that, over the years, only grew until it was deep enough in the subconscious to bury a whole family.

"Robles always sounded dreadful to me, son," the older man said. He sat back in the finished chair positioned square at the head of his dining room table. At the time, his house was still under construction. Freddy felt the draft from an opening in the ceiling.

"Dreadful, sir?"

"It reminds one of *rubble*." Hands steadily rotated a now lukewarm cup of coffee on its saucer, creating a light clinking sound of ceramics. Freddy watched his interlocutor work the cup with his hands and winced at the sound. The coffee undulated but never broke the confines of the rim. He noticed how white it looked, stirring in there. "Would you consider changing it?"

"*Change?*"

He knew he should have uttered that with more fire, to appear incensed, insulted at the idea of altering his name. Yet the bite left his tongue.

"Besides, when I leave the bar to you, it will make the transition that much cleaner." The older man reached across the corner of the table, placed a hand on Freddy's shoulder. "What do you think of that, *son?*"

Now looking into the rearview mirror, he saw the cityscape withdraw into the earth. He contemplated the city, and how he hasn't left Tiempo in quite some time. For a moment, he forgot the cardinal directions. 'No,' he thought, 'He stationed himself out north, because of course he would… But where is McAllen? Are we closer or further away from the Gulf? Would her body empty out into the Gulf…?"

Off in the distant plains, a gang of four spotted horses fed upon piles of hay behind yards of wired fence. Like most border cities over the decades, agriculture life was nearly extinguished, bought-up, and squeezed out to exist, if at all, as satellites along the northern edges. Freddy's lonesome Chevy cut through arid ranchland.

Busy hands continued peeling away at the steering wheel. Black flecks appeared on his palms.

The sun bore down upon the land, threatening to bend the cabin roof. Red waves of heat rose from the earth. Freddy turned, and the horses were one melted, multi-legged creature.

He wiped the sweat from his brow.

"Do you need some water, *mijo*?"

In a blink, Freddy stirred from his seeming reverie. A clock radio issued *noticias* sifted through static off in another room. Here, at the old Quintanilla's dining room, again, after so many years, Freddy recycled the last breath he took, as if it lingered in stasis for him. He felt a draft from above.

He didn't see the old man get up.

"Here you go," Quintanilla said, setting a glass of water for Freddy on the table. "You don't look so good."

The dining room was lit by the pulsating radiance of the sun breaking through the open front door down the hall and emanating from a window in the kitchen.

"Keeps getting hotter out there."

"Yes, well, that's something you and I cannot control," Quintanilla said, sitting down at the head of the table, at the exact same angle as before. "You seem consumed by something, *mijo*. Is everything okay at home? Beatrice and Lena are fine, aren't they?"

Freddy nodded his head. "Yes, they're fine."

"Lena—she doing good in school?"

"Yes."

"Good. To be honest with you, one has to have an eye on these schools, really any institution that abides by these affirmative action rules. I had my doubts—still do—about kids getting in because of this or that. Lena, I know, was raised right. Had both of you there. As sharp as her mother; and thank God she doesn't have your looks." He lightly punched Freddy on the shoulder; and as his laughter settled, said, "Bea was always lighter than you."

Freddy was on the last long draught of water at the last utterance, and nearly choked on it.

"But you are here for a reason, I suppose," the old man continued. "Tell me."

It was here, at the senior Quintanilla's determination, that Freddy steadily retold a story, the recounting of which he made with painstaking adherence to memory. (It must be recorded that he went so far as to recount this narrative detail his nephew told him now a month ago: "The sky was so clear that night, we never expected it to rain," Luis Ruiz admitted. "In the end, it washed us away from each other. I landed somewhere, near a well in some ruined building—on the other side. I don't know where she landed, or even if she is alive"—his voice cracked—"but I feel that she is. She would not die like that. After she saw Ama die still expecting *you...*") While he spoke, Freddy didn't look into his father-in-law's eyes, but at the light streaming in through the kitchen window across from him, behind the old man, whose face sat mostly in shadow as an effect of the light surrounding them, strong enough to cast some of its presence into the adjacent dining room.

"Why do you want to waste time over these people?" the old man said. His arms had folded above his paunch with finality.

"What?"

"You tell the story, son, as if you're so involved. Why, I bet that kid of your sister's just wanted to use you. In some way, they *all* want to use you. I say get the damn paperwork done, like you. You did the smart thing back then—"

"But things are different now, sir," Freddy interjected. "It isn't as easy for even Mexicans to come in. It takes *years* the correct way."

"Well, let it take *years*." The old man leaned forward. "You would be smart if you don't let this bother you. All those years back, when a white man offered me the chance to own property, to assimilate into this economy—I took it. It feels good to never have to look out for the wrong kind of trouble. I don't have an entire system working against me. I have some land. I am *here*. Never once looked back."

"But, s—" Freddy interrupted. "You can't say you're looking

forward."

"I'm looking *away*. You should do the same."

The buzzing radio static overcame the air as the old Quintanilla eased back into his chair.

"So, Lena's doing good, eh?" He began to turn the empty glass with one hand.

As Freddy started for the hallway that led to the front doorway, a voice called after him, saying, "You sure you don't need money?"

Money was far from Freddy's mind, however. When he quit the house he emerged into a reddening South, and, for a flash, all the land rolled in from four directions, sinking into him; all that dust and crash of stupid earth and stupid humanity burying him to the crown of his head, belching him out to reality once more, unfortunately. His truck seemed so far.

'One step at a time,' he thought; and as he walked under a wash of sweat, the voice of his nephew came to him over the horizon of Tiempo and memory:

"Some speak about an alternative to the river. I'm not sure if what they say is true, or even if it can be accessed; but some of us have started to cross *underground*, through tunnels. I found it hard to believe, but when it comes to escaping, I think nothing limits us.

"There is no river underground," Quintanilla remembered Luis saying.

Approaching the truck, he could discern the stampeding of

manifold hooves, clumsily eating the daylight between the plains and him. The breathing, harried and confused, as if divided into multiple airways, competed with the rhythm of melting hearts.

Over this cacophony of nothing, the thoughts occurred to him, that if spat out on the other side, Luis might opt for the tunnels, taking the chance underground. 'In the tunnels,' Freddy thought, 'That's where I've left my blood.'

LETTER TO HIS SON

Ultimately, he chose against calling for him.

'No need for anymore words,' Felix thought. 'I condemned him enough with words. It's all in the letter now; and those words will replace every single word before it. I never realized how hard it was to write. It was one of the hardest things.

'The old house. Writing brought me to the old house. To the time when I was a child but still ruined. Windows were always open. Gray and open, but it never rained. The weeds waved hello through the window. Sound of wings somewhere in the house. Round every corner. No sign of Mom or Dad. Every white doily on every table now dusty and brown. Sound of wings, yet no dust is lifted. Not a thing

166

disturbed. No language. Where is Mom and Dad. Look: I'm not speaking Spanish. Still no language. Outside there is someone circling the house. Weeds are so light on the body and do not disturb. They bend and wave and are broken. Round every corner. Can I play my music? No one's there to teach me. I can learn through ear. I can play a Steve Jordan tune. Finally: No one to disturb me while I play. I can play like *el huracan del valle*. No language. Where is the squeezebox? I want to drown the sound of wings. I can play like I play for my buddies after work. They sat greasy and drunk and waiting for my hand. Their faces are stretched and stretched in sadness. *they can't afford to leave to stay a house like this but why would they want one like this they must own the sound of wings round every corner*

'Thirsty… You think you can tell them to bring me some water? You, standing by the curtain…'

you cant hold it

'Oh, just a little.'

they said you cant hold it

'Can I hold you? Why are you so far by the drapes?'

why couldnt you say what you wrote before

'What can I say? I never learn. I couldn't with you.'

youve said a lot to me and i was expected to forgive you

'You let me back in. You didn't have to.'

i have a soft spot what can i say

'Why do you sound like waves?'

because you are guilty

'But you let me back inside. Why? I was draining you. I couldn't contribute like a man must. I was draining you.'

there is a wound

'I fucking know that. There's a desert in my mouth. I can't hold water. Bleeds more inside.'

a wound that gets stronger by water

'You gonna just stand there and tease me until… I don't have much longer do I…'

there was this other wound

'I know I know.'

travel the letter

'(Dear Tyler—*no* Dear Son *my son*—Dear Son I never wrote one of these my whole life, and now I can't remember a lot of things about writing. I remember going to school in the first or second elementary ever built in Tiempo. I remember writing my name in cursive within the lines and getting the stickers and learning about sentences and grammar and commas and stuff like that. I remember trying to write down something I heard my Tia say in Spanish and the teacher who didn't know a lick of Spanish corrected me just like my mother. For a time, I hated writing in English but I forgot Spanish after not having a reason to speak it. *youre trailing off* I'm not as good as you. I don't think anyone is as good as you. I've read every column you wrote. I think it's important that you know that. I can hear your voice and at the same time I can hear hers. You know how she talks. There is a lot of beauty and directness when she talks. I had no gift for words that you do. *no thats too much* I never understood why you took to writing. It's not a manly thing to pursue. Then again, what is manly anymore? I can't say I have acted like a man my entire adult life. Maybe to be a man is to have the walls around you your whole life until death pulls them from you so that you are finally free. But I will say your mother makes me forget about those walls sometimes. *there is a moth the size of my fist on my wall—write something that won't get you carried away if thats possible* I loved your mom *fuck but keep going* I really did. I still do. She and I met at the beach a long time ago over on South Padre on a day I tried marijuana for the first time and felt nothing behind those hills of sand off the side of the road. I was walking all lonely when I saw her reading some weird book about eyes and god by Zoro or someone. She liked the way people talked in the book, and I got her to read some of it to me and I could barely understand her but kept laughing and laughing mostly because of how stupid I felt. No one ever made me feel good to be stupid sometimes. Your mom really likes reading. I never met someone who goes to the beach with all that water in front of you just to read and get sand in the pages. She knocks me out. *it has eyes on its wings that cover the drapes* When she—I didn't know what to do. I didn't know how to raise a boy. I feel like I didn't. You are who you are because of you. You became a man all by yourself. No one told you to take care of this asshole, but you did it anyway. You saw things you should not have seen. You were too young to understand anything, but it was brought upon you like some sort of shitty inheritance. *go on to some place else Christ—(I call my mom but my voice echoes because there is no one in the house)—someplace else* I don't want to leave you alone son *fuck* But know that you are never alone. *fuck* Don't be like me. I know we never saw eye to eye. In time, you will because you have a piece of me in your memory. *it happened to me with your mom and my mom Christ i dont know if she is still alive—(it spreads its wings in the dark)—*I know you will see but you have to carry on and then it hits you. It hits you the way a clock ticks. You will remember me as a time and a place in your life and how you lived through it and look back on it. It always hits me in the time where your mom came home crying because they let her go from work. At the time, your mom was working two jobs because I had run up a bill on my credit card. I can't tell you where all that money went to. You tried your best to calm her down. You were just a kid back then. But you realized something went wrong and wanted to help. I remember that night because that was the first time I touched your mom in a while. That night, I held your mom like I held her when we were first in love, but things weren't the same between us. They never were. But at that time, it made sense to put my arms around her. *hair curly hair soft brown legs that go on and on smells like walking here there like sadness that you can smell tears that never went all the way down her face eyes like honeycombs i fell in love again i was always in love but i was also in my head and said the wrong words* I love you son. I remember the day she came back home with you. I didn't see her for a while because I said something stupid. But she took me back.

You were a smart kid but real shy. I tried my best to make you talk to me. You didn't even have to say dad. I didn't have a name yet. But you did. I still don't know where she got Tyler from but it fit, I think. *come on stop avoiding it* I'm sorry for saying the things I said. I really am. Not a day goes by where I don't think about it. If I could rewind the clock and not say those things… I should never have felt the way I did in the first place. I was just angry and confused. I was also jealous that you weren't mine. There is another wall of being a man is that you want children of your own blood, which I understand now is a foolish thing but it is what I felt then. I couldn't hold you like you were my boy. I bet you felt it too. I just hope you will think about that time and you will remember this letter. Let this be the last living thing you remember of me. If there's any room in your soul for me, let this be a part of it. *you have to stop now if you go on it will end where you dont want it to my mouth is getting dry again* I love you son. I will never leave you. I love you) I can't hold the water'

"W-Water."

"He's asking for water now," said a headless voice. "That won't help him now. They're going down."

"Just give it to him," said another.

"What does it matter?"

"That's why. Give it to him."

'God, you have made a desert and sea inside me.'

"Mr. Maldonado, can you hear us?" asked the second voice. "He's not responding."

"W-Water."

"I just gave him some."

"We're losing him."

"Should I call his family?"

"I think you should. By the time they get here, it might be too late."

| * |

It took fifteen minutes to drive on rain-slicked streets, the windows fogged by a wheezing heater that smelled of dust. Flor drove him. She didn't know what to say, and the choking smell didn't help produce words. She rolled down her window and drew a new breath.

After she dropped him off in front of the emergency, he rushed through dark lobbies and maze-like hallways. The unk-unk of his shoes followed him in soft echoes.

He almost lost his temper when he had to wait for the elevator guard to recognize that the person in front of him and that of the driver's license matched. Upward, to the ICU, down more hallways, turn the corner, another. Open the curtain. Notice the doctors at the EKG. They waited only to say something no one wanted to hear. Listen to the flatline that sounds like a concussion. It sings, unbroken. Take in the odor of bleach and urine and tears and mop water. Put it behind. Breathe through the mouth. It doesn't help. Walk slowly to him. Don't listen to their words. Look at the man lying asleep. His chest looks like it stopped full of the next breath.

He didn't wait for you.

172

The tapping starts. It's a meter. You don't hear it—

You inspect his hand, instead. There are grooves in the fingerprints that loop and run across the palm. The latter feels cool on your cheek. Gaze upon his closed eyes. It's easier now to look at him.

A woman with papers in her hands enters. She is dressed in black. She can finalize everything.

A G-chord wraps around you like an invisible robe, regal in its unknown hues—

Say, No. Feel something rattle in your throat. The urge to wail clutches your throat like a fire bathing a house. It constricts the tongue. It prevents swallowing.

You're still holding onto his hand.

"We found this underneath his pillow. It slid from beneath his head."

It's folded. It says "Tyler." You look down onto the paper and a small dark circle appears on it after you blink.

Why are you crying? Can't you see across the room where the beige curtains have dropped—there, underneath the shade of a jacaranda, swaying with a head full of leaves—there, leaning against the tree in the burgeoning cold that smarts the fingers holding a chord at the pearl teeth of a cream-colored accordion, a man, the near-exact likeness of the person lying in bed feet away, begins what might be the last song of his race on Earth? They don't play them like this anymore. No, sir. This is the song that does not dare outlast the extinguished spirit until the magma shawl that is for certain the final coffin abounds the weary, lonesome body. This is a song for a dying race whose threshing on the dancefloor can ease in somnolence. They stand now in the paleness of moonlight, dappled in that paleness, too, but still children of toasted maize, twirling now into the diagonal beam, and with them the old guards of culture which, at the tip of their spears, lanced at throngs of colonizers but also wedged inward to the mother of maize, the latter of whom—can't you see her?—beckons the dancers into her chest once cleft millennia ago by the Rio. She beckons the song master, himself, at last, reluctant to finish the ballad. In time, he acquiesces.

It isn't quite the wonder why you couldn't hear the song. It wasn't meant for your ears.

IN THE DARK, SHE TELLS THE STORY

She hated the neighbors because they didn't know. Maybe they did know—but only of the possibility. But how can you know for sure? One never knows until it's too late. The shell is tested before it is cracked and the yolk splatters and spills. She reeled her head back and realized how it all was a test of her fortress: the lowkey surveillance, the rooting through her phone, the discouragement from employment, the adherence to an older way of life, the tightening of a grip, the swing, the full swing. The yellowing vanity light coated the bathroom in a color close to vomit after a chicken soup dinner. About the air lingered light ribbons of roach aerosol that must have permeated, she assumed and hoped, most other mobile homes in her community. For some reason, she found pleasure in the thought of her neighbors being overrun by pests. She wanted to imagine them throwing a chancla *from the toilet of their home, maybe screaming in fear and fury. And yet they talked and talked somewhere behind the vomit-colored walls; and that talk was speckled with laughter.*

Tejano music reverberated in the bathroom window, the militaryesque snares sounding like the distant, trapped cymbals of her past. In the tub, she considered how long she could stay in that dry womb in which she sat before a roach poked its head from the drain.

She saw The Shining. *She knew what a man possessed could do. He could beat a woman because it's in his capacity to do so, and then go out to drink beer, party, befriend strangers, chanting and mimicking those mournful voices calling for her through the window. Still, she shuddered at the image of Rey's face protruding from the ax-stricken hole in the bathroom door; crazier-looking than Jack Nicholson, for she imagined foam dripping from his clenched jaw, and his eyes blanked, taking on the color of the bathroom interior.*

Everything surrounded her, even the spinning memories of who she is.

The bassline rambling outside, tickling her butt through the fiberglass tub, served as a meter to which her memory waked and danced...

I can still hear the gas burning underneath the pan, smell the blue fire underneath; still see what I thought I saw on it: a whole chicken on the fire, regaining its feathers. It must have been my imagination. Maybe the hissing steam from the water played tricks on my eyes. It was like when I was a little girl and I saw my grandma kill a chicken for the first time, but in reverse and in that steam like a ball of chalk. One by one, each feather unplucked. Like, it regained its head and everything. And instead of making me nauseous, it was possibly the most clear-minded I have ever been my whole life.

If only he didn't go through my messages. I thought I put my phone back in my bag. Why would he go through it anyway? Why *wouldn't* he? He keeps trying to know my business 24/7. So what if I message some guy more than I talk to him? Well, I guess that's what they call emotional cheating. But when you're getting the walls placed around you, your heart wants to go out. It wants to escape. Could I have been honest? I guess. But sometimes dishonesty is the only way we can fight back. Deceit is the guard.

I wonder if he knows him.

It's funny. They say everyone knows everyone down here. That might have been true at a certain time. Now, the Rio Grande Valley's opened up. There are more businesses on Main than ever before. Everyone's online now. I think it's even easier to become a stranger in Tiempo these days. You can live anonymously, and people think that's always a good thing...

What does Rey know about me? I mean, *really* know about me?

He didn't think I'd react the way I did. *I* didn't even see that coming.

Did I hit him too hard?

I haven't heard him move around since I ran in here.

But he didn't let go. I knew what was in store for me. He was grabbing me again. He had this tired look about him, like a dog limping off the road. He looked injured. He looked angry that he was injured. Looking at me like I had done it to him, like I was twisting some invisible knife into him. Like I was there holding him in place.

It's funny. I feel like humming.

I need to get out of this room. I don't know why I ran here of all places. I coulda run outside. I remember the restroom was the place I would run to whenever my parents started arguing and I thought it was my fault. It's always your fault when you're a kid. I would just sit in the tub, like right now, and cry waiting for someone to take me out the window. Like Barney or Selena or someone. My grandmother. I'd sit here and start humming. I wouldn't feel so alone, then.

Why do they have to have the music so loud? I'm tired of the same old sad songs. Even if they're singing about something happy, they sound sad as hell. Give the voice to someone else. Not me, though. I'm just stuck in a tub, and I can smell the mesquite burning in the pit outside, and the onion—and the fajitas. What a weird time to be hungry…

—so how did you get out of there?

—what

—you said you were in the tub, but then you kinda trailed off into food

—well, it smelled good. i can't help that.

—yeah, but it doesn't help me, especially right now. why don't you start with your escape. tell it as if you're telling those neighbors of yours.

—you really wanna spoil the mood and get me mad? i don't find use for that sometimes. there is a time and a place for that.

—did you want the light on?

—no. i want it this way. i want to give the effect of the conscience thinking what i'm about to say. like you yourself are thinking this.

—is that the weed talking?

—i don't know, but let me hit it one more time. imagine your mind as it really is: some darkness cradled in a skull. there are walls. but there's a spark that contains everything. it can create a floor so you know where your feet are and a ceiling so you know your head will hit something if you jump too high. take that spark and creep with me: you're fresh out the pussy and—

—whoa, there. where'd that come from?

—why you always gotta interrupt? thought you'd like that. your friends are kinda bad influences. anyways: you're fresh out the pussy, and it so happens you're born a girl. despite whatever bullshit your parents are going through, they manage their best to raise you as their little princess. in fact, everything from when you're a newborn all through childhood is a deliberate choice to make sure you know you're a girl. the clothes, the way you're told how to interact with other children, especially the boys, the way your hair's supposed to be, the aspirations you're supposed to at the very least start dreaming about. down to the toys they give you. you watch a lot of television. you wonder why certain characters react the way they do to something done to them. isn't it silly, you say, can't they call their mom and dad? grownups are silly to you. you tell your mom and dad how grandpa was being silly with you. there's shouting across the house, but you don't have to see grandpa again. dad holds you and buries his face in your hands. his cheeks feel like dolphins you pet at the aquarium once. his lashes are weird and shaky like what you think a daddy-long-legs' legs would be. he is your size.

    —then your body changes. parts of it seek to hurt you because of packaging, your mom tells you. why did god deliver us to the world like this, you ask her. you start to hate your body because it both wants to hurt you and hurts itself. your mother warned you, but hearing doesn't prepare you enough. you pray to another mother, god's *sancha*, but she can only keep her eyes closed because she's praying, too. you wonder do you always have to pray with your eyes closed reaching into darkness like that, like now, and you bow to her and leave. you want to leave your body. you don't develop as fast as other girls. the kids at high school make fun of you because they see music videos, they see reality tv, they turn on the mexican weather report, and they laugh because you don't look like that. not that you don't look like a hot white girl on tv; but that you don't look like a hot latina on tv, either. but you have seen their tias, their sisters, their mothers, and none of them look like the women on tv. you cry in your mom's embrace because she's the most beautiful woman you've ever seen and she's not commercial pretty. you feel sorry for yourself because it feels like you can't control anything. you move on from high school and come to a few realizations. one, the world outside school is very different. two, there are some qualities that remain the same. you begin to understand that you're part of a generation living through some truly unprecedented times. the internet, social media, influencers—all of this attracts you, and yet, there's something about it that still reminds you of things outside your control. there is a market for the image, and the image—again, doesn't look like you. go on because time goes on. you breathe a second away. fall for a guy who works as security at a middle school. he desires to protect these kids, and you admire that—you know, someone who really desires to do something must mean something to you. he seems like a good guy. he really sold you, or maybe bought you, on his wanting to protect those kids, kids that are in the middle of everything, because sometimes everything is simply split between childhood and adulthood. he keeps saying how he doesn't want them to change, doesn't want them to grow older; keeps listing names of all these kids balancing themselves on a curb waiting for the school bus to come. he knows them all, you think. you think it's admirable.

 —(keep creeping.) you think it's admirable, but as you go along with him for a year, you think his thinking might be a little off. you don't know if he knows that it's useless thinking. there's no such thing as always being a child when you're in school. you wonder if he's a child. after the first year he starts doing this thing, and it kinda catches you off guard at first, because you're used to seeing it followed up by something else, something more brutal, in movies. or you hear it from friends or family. so-and-so got beat by him. and wouldn't you guess it, she's still with him. but he never hit me. it was all in this one act, yet everything you thought you knew about him drops like curtains to a play and freezes in the back of your mind in images and color like a sad display at the mall. you wonder if he's capable of doing more. but it's something small. you trick yourself by calling it kinda cute that that's him at his worst. despite everyone telling you you're a dumbass, you move in with him, thinking it'll get better. it doesn't. it happens more often. each time you don't know what you've done; and there's nothing you could have done. you see, he's a product of another type of packaging. he's been brought up by other influences, the same ones that keep you out of their stories. you feel a sympathy for him. you laugh because you feel that way. you wonder if there's a way he can redeem himself, not through god, and not with you. but you stay because it's now been a few years and the walls have been drawn up and you haven't actually—i mean actually talked with your parents or your friends, and you start to wonder if they know. you try to find refuge where and when you can. you find it in the tub of the restroom, at the mall with your friends who tell you you should leave his ass, with a nice boy who gets you talking about things you like talking about—you find refuge anywhere outside of his knowing. how long will it last? until he becomes rich and successful in this little corner of the world? you think of his sister and how even she advises you to get the hell outta there. why do you stay? when will you leave? will you take your things? will he try to stop you? what's stopping you? think to run. no. run.

—you hit him with the pan you're reheating leftovers with. you hear it drop to the floor after a sizzling; and you wonder if the sizzle was the sound of the hot pan and his face momentarily meshing into one. it drops and you run, but you don't immediately know where, so you wind up going to the room you hide yourself in when your parents used to fight. he bangs at the door a few times, tries to twist the handle until it seems useless. he quits and you sit in the white tub you think looks like an egg. you can still hear the gas burning in the kitchen. you know he won't turn it off, so you kinda wait until the house burns down. it doesn't. you're still in your egg. you feel like drowning yourself. imagine how peaceful it might be, to fill your lungs with shitty Tiempo water, water you've seen people on facebook light on fire from the faucet. you would have a potential fire in you.

—you hear the front door creak open and slam. that's when you know it'll be safe to go to your room, get some things, and take off through the back. you start packing, and you wonder, where do i go? you don't think to go back to your parents. you haven't told them a goddamn thing since you left, and it would be too much of a braid to untangle. you think about your friends, but you hesitate. you think about how many times you try to contact them and all of them are either busy or just don't respond when you want them to. so you go to a boy's house, hoping he would open his door at two o'clock in the morning and not criticize you or tell you things you don't want to hear, only for him to do all of this, but you do most of the talking. it's dark in his room. you face him in bed. it feels like you're whispering into a chink in the wall, hoping it'll crumble after you're done telling it what you need to tell. you feel like you are a child, a teen, and the woman you are all at once. everything feels new, lying in someone else's bed. you start feeling bad about the way you talked about your neighbors and their music. if anything, you wanted to join them and sing with them and tell their daughters they're beautiful and go shot for shot with their brothers and idle by the pit and finally learn how to barbecue because that's something kept from you.

    —you think about the story you just told. think about how it happened and how you told it. do they match up? things are lost. you can't piece everything together. that's not authentic. the telling is. but you feel you didn't do a character justice. you wonder, does he need justice? you think, probably, but that's not my story. my story's always moving.

| * |

    Tyler's such a strange name. I wonder if he knows that. It's a strange name for a person like him down here, like he was whitewashed at birth.

    Things are quiet after the story. I kinda don't want him to say

184

anything. I just want to lay here for a while, to listen to the passing cars. Main Street's just a backyard away.

I can feel him thinking. It's kinda funny. Off down that way, I can feel something unsettled and maybe forever so. And right next to me in the soft breathing, I can feel him thinking.

Will he take all of them from the shelf and leave with them? How would they do in a car for that long? I've heard him complain about how they warp in the sun. There's one that I know he borrowed from the library—I think it's called, *Time Enough*—he told me he has no intention of returning it. I said whatever. His rebellions.

You never know exactly what he thinks, but you know it takes something out of him; and I don't know if it places it back, if it can even come back. Can something be taken from you—like *deep* from you—without it coming back in some way?—in the same way? No, it can't come the same way. Never.

"The weed left me a while ago," he says.

"Me too."

Things seemed to settle. The night outside sounds like listening, like a patient reception, the slow wheeling to the earth. It's funny. I think it wants to rain.

The springs of the bed creak. I can tell them apart: his shadow sitting upright and the dark room around him.

"Wanna get drunk at the Worm?"

| * |

"Where's Q.?"

185

Pablo's at the bar. New guy that took Luis's place. I remember Luis wearing that apron.

"Out back. He's got something cooking."

Tyler looks at me, taking a few sniffs from the air, like a dog. Behind him, high on the wall, there's that photograph taken here—well, they all are—of her in her later years before the cancer took her. That wide set of pearls across her mouth. She looks like Selena when she smiles. There's this confidence behind the eyes. They watch her people—her children dance and know of the intoxication of life, of the grief and the injury, maybe even the cancer, and then there's the dancing and watching her children twirl like flowers blooming in fast-forward to her songs. There's a timelessness in her knowing gaze, *la reina de los boleros*.

I follow Tyler as we head out through the back door. She follows me.

Outside Q. has this little food operation. There's this dude at a barbeque pit turning chicken quarters over the glowing coal. Q. is head at an assembly line putting away the chicken in Styrofoam plates, while to the side of him a handful of people grab from various Tupperware rice and beans.

"Different people made each," I hear Q. tell Tyler. I know Tyler probably wants to talk with him, so I linger.

It's five others making the plates. They're having their own conversation.

"Are you sure you don't want *someone* to teach them a lesson?

I know some guys…" one of them said. I couldn't tell if they were playing around.

"No, no," another answered. Her eyes were busy with bean portions. Purple rims above her lashes. Hands in sheer plastic gloves—all of theirs were. "If I could break the bones of everyone who's wronged me, then…" She looked up like she was counting all of her enemies. "Hello!" she caught herself. "I wasn't just contemplating violence!" She gave me a sly smile. I just noticed her throat. It wasn't the shape of a vase, or not a smooth one, at least. It looked knotted-up.

"Hi! Don't mind me. I was just casually eavesdropping. Mind if I join?"

There was a couple at the end next to the one with the purple eyeshadow. They let me put the plates into a big cardboard box. Next to us with its trunk open, someone reversed their SUV. There's a gentle something about everything. A softness that's hard to point out.

"What are these plates for—and so late at night?" I asked. My question didn't disrupt the movement of hands.

"They're sheltering some asylum seekers over at Tiempo Basilica downtown," said the man to the right of the woman with purple eyeshadow. He wore a backwards cap and a tight-fitting T-shirt that looked like a uniform. "We just got the news—or Julia over here got the news this afternoon."—he nodded toward the woman next to him—"Would've been more here, I guess. It was pretty last-minute."

I looked at Q. still talking with Tyler.

"Kind of a weird place to do this," I said.

"I guess," the guy answered. "He sought *us* out, actually."

"He said he saw one of our posts," Julia said. "We do this once a month; twice if we have the people and the resources. It's not easy getting people out of their bubble and cooking or donating what they got. Sometimes people feel so small and helpless when all it takes sometimes is showing up."

She looked up to me again with the shade of violet behind her lashes. I couldn't help but to detect a sense of sadness in her face. She made the connection and met my eyes; but they subtly withdrew, like someone had opened a door in another room, and the curtains shifted, and there was a shadow that hasn't entered yet. Like she was expecting someone and shrunk in it. In the expectation.

They continued talking. It was a nice low hum. The dude next to Julia—his name is Raul, or Suave. The other three make fun of how much he goes to the gym. (He complained once that his arms were tired assembling all the plates, and the rest of them went, "NAAHHHH!") The other two are quiet, to themselves, a couple. They share that intimate closeness, the kind that says you're never in the way. They move like two shadows of the same body. Mauricio and Laly. There's a slight pause when they momentarily touch.

The girl, Erica, speaks. "You know, you can stay at our place if you feel like you can't go home."

What?

"No, girl. I don't want to put you out." She wasn't talking to me. Julia seemed harried in her movement after she answered. "I'll just go back to my parents for the meantime. Sure, my dad won't like it. He still hasn't *seen* me."

"I'm sorry to interrupt, but what happened?" I asked.

"Oh, nothing," Julia said. "Little boy problems. You try to be as straightforward as possible,"—she never lifted her eyes from her work—"explain things to the best of your knowledge, because—and I know it's weird—you, yourself, don't know everything that's happening to you—you just know you're getting closer to something more authentic—but people throw pebbles. There's only so many times that the homeboys can call you *joto* before you start questioning whether the person you're sleeping with is really a girl. That's all it ever was, girl. Little boy problems."

It's funny. I hadn't seen a fly near the table until now.

"Yeah, but he still didn't have to react the way he did," Suave said. He plopped the beans onto the plate with emphasis, as if punctuating his statement.

Q. has his back to us, minding the pit with the other guy, who from this angle looks like an older gentleman, like a *tio*. At some point minutes ago, Tyler's phone buzzed. He's in the alley talking with someone.

"I guess we can take a break, guys," Julia said, peeling her gloves off. "I have to go to the restroom."

"Sounds good. Y'all won't believe it, but this has been giving me a real good workout."

Suave's friends all rolled their eyes, even Julia who started walking back into the bar.

I went to Q. to see what was up with Tyler.

"Some serious call," he said. "Wouldn't be surprised if it was the hospital."

The pit stood there dark and open. He still had some quarters to cook. I asked him if he could teach me how to grill. He told me I was too late for the fire, but to get him an onion from the kitchen.

I sprang into the bar and bypassed Pablo on his phone, into the kitchen and plucked an onion from the walk-in. On my way out, before pushing the door for the back exit, I heard what sounded like muffled crying in the women's restroom.

Maybe I shouldn't.

The door to the women's restroom looks like a vault. I knock on it, but I barely hear it. The muffled sound persists. From outside, I could hear the group laugh. They probably didn't know.

The door isn't so subtle. It squeaked the entire way open. I'm inside and Julia's at the sink daubing her eyes with a brown paper towel.

"I'm sorry," she said. "I know it's across the hall." She didn't look at me.

"No, you're fine. Are you okay in here? Your eyeshadow's running."

"Fuck. You spend so much on this crap… Fuck." She met eyes

with herself in the mirror. "I'm a mess." She kinda laughed as she became more precise in daubing the paper towel around the corners of her eyes. Before long she reevaluated her look. I noticed her neck again. We met eyes. "It's really noticeable, isn't it? All this stuff is really expensive. Sometimes things have to remain there for a while."

"It looks bruised."

"Oh. Yes, I guess it does. Happens when you're an imposter."

"Imposter? All I see is a girl readjusting her makeup."

I wasn't expecting the hug. It felt like years of getting lost in Amá's nightgowns.

"Thank you for being here," Julia said.

The yellow onion grew sweaty in my hand. I held onto it behind her back. Q. told me it was to clean the grill, so I didn't want to let go.

WHAT HE WRITES

I.

In the bus seat, he attempts to balance his pencil on his left index finger, the rolling asphalt underneath him and the climb out of the Rio Grande Valley jeopardizing the balancing act.

In the bus, he begins to scribble on a yellow legal pad. NO ONE EVER LEAVES YOU.

He contemplates the traveling window.

A window shows you that there's an outside. That there's perhaps a structure you're inside of; but there's the outside.

Will there be a window outside Tiempo that I can gaze

through? There must be—that's obvious. We get viewed so many times during election season, picked up and investigated like a *tlacuache* in the hands of pest control, with our hands up and our tails taut. People give us meaning, outside. They ascribe characteristics. They use words like Volatile, or Deadly, or Uneducated, or Liminal.

Liminal, it seems to me, is a trick we've played on ourselves. We've adopted it and say it with pride. When our own in this liminal space abide by the same laws, exhibit the same behavior as the people who drew the lines they told us not to cross, what's the point in being liminal? If some of our own people perpetuate and maintain those vicious stories, what's so special about being at the center of a diagram? So many of us cling to this idea and work within it and get shit pay in it and treat our women poorly in it and perform violence in it and stir around in its confines not realizing we're drowning. I may as well be writing about time and place: These are the main self-serious culprits that have effectively transformed into wounds forever widening. Some are right to level their complaints at borders. You're out, I'm in. Someone owns this, another owns that. How long are these boundaries maintained by those in power? Long enough to extinguish our memory, then our spirit. Yes, time and place. Inescapable. And so we must lie to ourselves and perform the liminal as if that is our muscle. We were *caught* in-between. We grew in the cracks like a flower pushing out from the wall's foundations, wishing we were trees.

What is the cure to these self-inflicted wounds?

I can't help but to think about the stories I've heard in my time, in Tiempo. I wish that could translate into making my own. Sooner or later, I find myself writing about someone I know. It then becomes a pseudo-biography or -fiction. You spend enough time with someone and their personality bleeds into and mixes with yours. There's no way that I'm me only. I'm my parents; I'm Flor and Rey; Willie David, Diego; Q. and… I'm this woman across the aisle from me wearing at least three layers of clothing and a blanket reading what looks like some gigantic Webster, those you pick up for $5 at a used bookstore. I'm her tearing out a word and placing it in an inner pocket of her purse, retrieving some cards and laminates from the same pocket, fumbling with them as the bus stutters to a stop.

(A baby's crying somewhere in the bus.) It had been an hour since we left McAllen.

An hour since we left McAllen and I'm not her anymore. I'm not her being asked questions, being asked to stand up, being taken by the arm and told to stand. I'm not the one saying, Sympathy, Sympathy, down the narrow path of onlookers watching out of periphery. I'm not the invisible one being vanished. I'm not the expired one. I won't be the one going back to Tiempo, or wherever they go, though it is Tiempo, only underneath Tiempo. I am not the one truly without a land, beneath the land

"hey."—i'm standing in the middle of the aisle now—"why are you taking her away?"—what am i doing.—the Uniform at the

steps turns toward me.—i feel their eyes behind the sunglasses.—
don't men-in-black me.—the woman looks to me, my mother in her
smile, everyone's mother in her smile.—she shakes her head.—the
Uniform shifts her aside the walkway.—she tugs on the Uniform's
sleeve, bypasses them, walks the line toward me.—she outlines my
face with silk palms—bootsteps—"*Con tiempo*"—bootsteps…

Here I thought I was leaving a border town. I suspect every
and any place I visit will be a border town. Fragmented.

I'm seated, again. Placed there by a firm hand.

The crying is finally getting to me.

There's a carousel starting

and it's—here it goes—people perpetually taking a seat across
the aisle—the woman sitting back down with her Webster—she's
holding out a torn piece of language—I'm sorry I don't know
RESPONSIBILITY—Can anyone describe the word
RESPONSIBILITY to me?—Is it something i can control—Don't go,
mama—i can see her tuck and roll onto the outside reel of road
underneath pink milk sky—she'll be back—Flor takes the seat next—
she shows me where the bruises are—i'm so sorry Flor—had i known
you before everything—Why didn't you come with me—she walks
out of frame—Can someone get that baby—wiping sweat off my
forehead—bootsteps—there are tiny purple trumpets blowing by like
they have all the time in the world—Can anyone hear me—i look up
to the seat in front—up pops the half face of Old Crow—no words—
the walkway and the window keep alternating—Am I the one

rotating—Diego sits across from me now—Oh Diego, please tell me what's going on—It's pretty apparent, bro—What do you mean—bootsteps—You should know, *ese*—You're the one leaving—Thanks for the car, by the way; I'll take good care of it—Diego, does it feel like everything is going fast fast fast out of your hand?—You are not the one who is disappearing—can't you see Diego—look at my hands—the purple flowers like a tapestry—i can't see my hands—i hold my invisible hands to my face and cover my eyes—bootsteps—i haven't eaten anything and it's coming up—nothing's coming up—

"Hey man," calls a voice from above me. "Are ya okay?"

I was too busy meshing my cloistering hands together in front of me, torso bent over. They must have felt my head bump into their seat when I returned from the restroom.

"I'm okay now." I didn't want to be bothered.

"Hey man, I heard ya heavin' in there."

I lifted my head to see who terrorized me with words. Some old dude with pink flared nostrils, blue eyes, a cotton weave of white hair setting above unkempt brows like perfect clouds. I couldn't see his mouth as he spoke.

"Hang in there. I hear the next stop is coming real soon. Falfyurious, I reckon?" His eyebrows raised. "I've been working on my Texas accent? Ya reckon?—"

"Does it look like I want to talk, sir?"

"Well, I just thought you needed some company, y'know?" I could barely discern a mouth moving past the gap between the seats.

I couldn't help but to imagine some odd reason he never raised his face completely, like maybe he only had one tooth in his mouth, or maybe a goiter. "My name's Gary. I'm on my way back to Los Angeles—the one in California. Was visiting some relatives down here in your Valley."

Outside. It's so gray and bright. The sky is full of silver linings.

The bus had hissed and stopped. I took the open seats a couple left—away from that guy. Why couldn't he take a hint?

Across the aisle is this greasy old dude…

II.

The bus station received another suspirating metal horse with stuttering engine like a broken toy. All lanes under the garage were occupied save for one meant for emergency stops, for journeys never meant to stall. The shade nulled the gentle chrome sheen from a soft sun.

All heads popped up from either above the seats or aside toward the aisle in anticipation, trying to glean the visage of the driver. No one could ever see anything underneath the glossy nose from the rearview mirror above his head, so when the voice came over the passengers' heads the second time, they could hardly believe that such an erudite voice came from a person. Some whispered to another that they thought the voice was coming from a bilingual automation, perhaps at the press of a button.

The aisles kept quiet as a woman with a clipboard climbed the steps into the bus once it parked. The plexiglass partitioned the conversation the two had under the steady snoring of the engines surrounding. The woman never consulted the clipboard pressing against her uniform, stamping over her paunch rounding the crotch of her pants. Laughter cut through the groaning engines, followed by the woman quitting the bus.

"All right, folks," came the voice through the overhead intercoms, "Those with connecting buses here, consult your tickets to know which ones you have to be on. If you were not supposed to change buses, we are going to locate another one for you to take you the rest of the way." The driver rose from his seat, nearly bumping his head on the ceiling. The yellow vest hung from his lanky body, the bones underneath salient under the brown skin. "Welcome to San Antonio."

The downtown bus station teemed with clamor and phone chargers guarded by shifty eyes. It's all *going* in this place. At the "phone charging station," a woman presses her phone to her ear with her bare shoulder. A bus driver sitting across from her eyes her thin lips as they split open to reveal clenched teeth, saying, "I am *here*. Where are *you*? Well, you better get down here quick if you want to make it in time." She discovers the man glancing over at her. "This place gives me the creeps." Over on the other side of the station, a man places with the care of a dynasty servant a coffee can from two plastic H-E-B bags, one bag reinforcing the other, on the ticket counter. The contents of the can rattle like raw shifting beans diving into the crockpot. "I need to get somewhere," he says, spilling blackened change in a pool of dull shine. The rolling suitcases gliding over cement, sounding every crack and bump, never ceases, never crescendos. Eyes always stuck to the clock on wrists, televisions mounted high, cell phones, the ticket clerk announcing arrivals and departures. The ticket clerk lifts the phone connected to the intercom system to announce departures, but his attention is drawn elsewhere: off to the side, in a group of travelers clutching revised transit schedules on their tickets, a man suddenly stood and began to pace in front of a bench. His white flesh reddened, the white of his beard a hard contrast to it. Along the underside of his chin ran a tapestry of moles, crowned and brown, bubbling from beneath the white flesh. From the breast pocket of his jean shirt, he produces a notepad and pen.

"Last summer I visited my aunt, and she told me everyone's leaving," the man said. "Oh, but the Valley is such a beautiful place, especially San Antonio-side."—he began to scribble on the notepad— "I've been jotting down notes on my little trip here. Texas, it seems, isn't a lost cause. National talk makes it out to seem like everyone's shooting the place up. The West full of bullet-holes!"

"The violence isn't always blatant"—a voice almost indirect, from a body lounging on the bench before the man pacing.

"I don't know about that, man. Quiet"—he began dictating

words he scrawled onto his pocket-sized notepad, giving him the silhouette of some hard-boiled detective piecing together clues—"Quiet were these beaten streets. Streets that run indiscriminate like the mother of the Valley, the Rio herself." The man smiles after dotting the end of his thought.

"The Rio is always someplace mystical. People build myths and legends from 'her'. It's *brutal*."

"What do you mean by 'brutal'?"

"Never mind."

"You're the most cynical Texan I've met yet! Are you sure you're alright? You've looked nauseous for a long time." The person on the bench fell silent, skin blanching, back slumped forward, face indistinguishable. A bus with its tail-end submerged in the cavernous moiling shade, reflected an undivided shard of white sun into the station from a metallic panel of its head. The sheet of light casted its silklike body onto the face of the person sitting on the bench, never broken by the writer sidestepping its angle. "Hey, man, sorry but you gotta lighten up a bit. Ever since we left that city—well, I don't know if you can call that a city—*Temple*, right?—anyway, you've been like this for a while after. Was that your home? Eh, I wouldn't worry about it. You're a smart enough kid."—he taps the person's head with a light finger—"It'll all be fine. Just forget about it."

"Forget about it?"

"Yeah, you can control it, can't you? From here on out you can be a world traveler, like one of those beatniks that live from city to city, never quite knowing where or who they are. That's what this bus is for, isn't it? To *go*. Not being in a place long enough. Not knowing anyone." He trailed off in thought and resumed writing. To him the notepad allows him definition. All things are set in his writing. The surrounding crowd, initially inattentive to their conversation, steadily grew interested, eyes acknowledging their presence via periphery, creating a cursory tapestry of clipped eyes.

"Well, the least I can own is the knowing of the people I knew. They are my memory." The person on the bench lifted their head, though any eye from the crowd could sparsely see the face that addressed the writer pacing like a busy pendulum. They heard as the person spoke of people they never heard of: of a dude that went to a park to check out naked women protesting; of a boy disappeared; of a woman choosing to reinvent herself in a culture that needed to keep up with her; of a writer unable to find comprehension, nor acceptance from the Valley. Whoever that person was, they referred to a place— constantly returning to this *place*, not as some abstract word that might encompass these lives they spoke of, but as an *actor*, a character in a play with the backdrop of itself, its psychology reaching outward the proscenium arch.

They spoke to the deaf ear of the writer creating a meter with his footsteps. The watchful crowd noticed a sadness blended in the voice's inflections. Some recognized the voice as the voice of their cousin, or perhaps a brother they hadn't seen in a while. There was a streak of stressful humanity in the speech.

The voice from the bench stopped with the abruptness of a needle being lifted from a record. No one could tell whether the writer still pacing was writing from his own thoughts, or if he was endeavoring to copy the speech. The person on the bench lifted their bus ticket, contemplating it. He then rose from the bench and walked toward the reception counter.

The eyes from the crowd followed the speaker from bench to counter. From the counter, they pointed outside, undoubtedly through the long windows opening out to the corral of buses. They rushed out with an amended ticket, out until the body became enveloped in light quitting the station. As a man with a burgundy suit, golden crucifix in hand, replaced the person on the bench before that swaying writer, some from the crowd thought to tell their siblings, their spouses, parents about the person they had heard that day, and how they were reminded of their family, but no one knew the name of the person, nor could they with certainty say they ever saw their face. Neither could they discern from their memory the name of that town—city?

Max Tyrone Lozano is a poet and novelist from the Rio Grande Valley. His work centers around the everyday lives of people living on the southern Texas-Mexico border. His poems have featured in *Gallery*, *Rigorous,* and *samfiftyfour*. *Tiempo, Texas* is his debut novel.

9 798218 595456